The Other Boyfriend

SYLVIA MASSARA

License Notes

This novel is entirely a work of fiction. The names, characters, and incidents portrayed in it are the work of the author's imagination. Any resemblance to actual persons, living or dead, events, or localities is entirely coincidental.

Published by Tudor Enterprises
Australia
(61) 419 492 623

This eBook Edition 2016
First published by
Tudor Enterprises in 2010, 2013

ISBN: 978-0-9875475-2-1

DEDICATION

This book is dedicated to the indomitable Rosepurple. You are every day missed and never forgotten!

Titles by Sylvia Massara

Romantic comedy:

Like Casablanca
The Other Boyfriend

General fiction:

The Soul Bearers

Mia Ferrari mystery series:

Playing With The Bad Boys
The Gay Mardi Gras Murders
The South Pacific Murders

Sci-fi Romance:

The Stranger

For more information on Massara's novels, both in eBook
& paperback editions, plus participating retailers;
or for latest novels or to contact the author, please visit:
www.sylviamassara.com

CHAPTER 1

A large window behind Monica revealed panoramic views of the city of Hong Kong, and though I tried to appreciate the beauty before me, it didn't work. *Nothing worked!* I was in the grips of an anxiety attack brought on by desperation. All I could think about was Jeffrey with his de-facto partner, Moira—the ball and chain as I called her—living in a loveless relationship until the end of time. And as far as I was concerned, the end of time was a long way away.

"Sarah, let me get this straight," Monica exclaimed in disbelief, taking a deep drag from her cigarette. "You want me to help you find a boyfriend for your lover's partner?"

I smiled weakly at my best friend. I couldn't blame her incredulity at what I was proposing. I hardly believed it myself so how could I expect someone else who was obviously sane, unlike me, to believe it?

Monica took another drag from her cigarette and expelled a cloud of smoke that momentarily obscured my view of her face. I squirmed at the thought of what she was making of all this while I reached for the red wine she had offered earlier and gulped it down, almost choking in the process. Meanwhile, my mind filled with agonising thoughts about the uncertain future of my relationship with my lover, and I hoped against hope that somehow a miracle would bring us together for good.

Jeffrey had told me repeatedly that he didn't want to hurt Moira's feelings by dumping her after fifteen years of being together. But staying with her in what was obviously a platonic relationship for the sake of pity was just crazy. I fumed every time I thought about it.

It was unbearable. Jeffrey should be with me by now. I squeezed my eyes shut for a moment and prayed for that elusive miracle.

"Mike!" I was brought out of my reverie by Monica's excited cry.

"What?" I asked, somewhat confused, briefly entertaining the idea that she had lost her mind. Perhaps, the heavy smoking had finally taken its toll on her, and she couldn't think straight anymore. *What's this about a mike?*

Monica crushed the cigarette butt into a large crystal ashtray, already overflowing with the remnants of other cigarette butts that had met the same fate. "Mike!" she exclaimed in exasperation, frowning at me.

Like I'm supposed to know what she's talking about. I hoped against hope that she wasn't thinking of a karaoke microphone. *Heaven forbid.* This was what happened to expats when they lived in Asian countries for too long.

Another large gulp from my refilled wine glass and I was ready to focus on what she was trying to say. "Who or what is 'mike'?" I asked, trying to hide my impatience. As she lit up another one of those little deadly cylinders I hated so much, the thought crossed my already tired mind that I was going to have to wash my hair in order to get rid of the horrible, clinging smell of smoke. I sighed.

Monica rolled her eyes at me. "Honestly, Sarah, you really don't remember?"

No, I don't remember. I had no idea what she was going on about, but it was obvious that some diabolical scheme was forming in her fag-fogged brain because whenever she was excited about something, her British accent became more pronounced.

The view of the busy harbour faded in and out before my eyes while Monica puffed away furiously. I waited, hoping this was just a weird dream I was having; and if luck was on my side, I'd soon wake up and things would be normal once more. Or worse still, I thought in alarm, I really was drunk in some karaoke bar, and it was my turn to sing. *Oh please, God help me!*

"Mike's the man for the job," Monica announced between puffs. I paid full attention. "You know him," she went on. "He's been living here for five years—investment banker from London. You met him at my last Christmas party."

I had a vague recollection of Monica's Christmas party, all of it through an alcoholic haze. My blank stare must have registered through the smoky lounge room because she sighed and said, "Never mind," dismissing my look of ignorance. "The thing is that Mike's always up for a challenge, and I know he'll love this." She threw me a mysterious smile.

"And how do you know?" Despite the fact that I was convinced her cigarettes were impregnated with some sort of hallucinogen, this managed to pique my curiosity.

"Because he's gorgeous and he's never had to chase a single female in his life. Women fall all over him," she explained as if I were too slow to understand her meaning.

Poor Mike, I rolled my eyes. Life was sooooo tough for some people! But if women really did fall all over him, as Monica suggested, this might just work. I felt the stirrings of hope for the first time since my arrival in Hong Kong. "Okay," I found myself saying as if we were simply planning an outing rather than scheming to change a person's entire life. "This so-called lady killer sounds perfect, but how do you know he'll do it?"

Monica crushed her cigarette butt into the ashtray. "Because he's transferring to Taipei next month and he'll be bored to tears unless he's got something like this to occupy him."

Charming! I couldn't wait to meet this male version of a femme fatale. Yet, Monica seemed so sure about him that I almost believed this man could be the solution to my problem. "So how do we know he's going to find Moira attractive?" I didn't want to give way to my rising excitement just yet, not to mention the fact that Moira might find the guy totally repulsive.

"That isn't the point, dummy. If Mike says he'll do it, then he'll do it," Monica replied, full of confidence.

"But if he's not attracted to her, why would he waste his time charming the woman in order to help someone he doesn't even know? Besides," I countered, "Moira might hate the sight of him." Doubt and reality set in and I saw my dream of a free Jeffrey fading quickly away.

Monica laughed as if the thought of someone finding her precious Mike unattractive was outrageous. "In answer to your question, Mike owes me for a past favour, and I know he'll do it if I ask him. As for Moira, the minute she lays eyes on him, she's toast," she reassured me, reaching out and absently patting my arm.

I decided to keep an open mind about Moira's reaction to

"God's gift to women". I certainly did not need to ask Monica what kind of favour she had done for Mike in the past. Monica had always had a way with men. One look at her luscious blonde hair and attractive features that matched an equally luscious figure said it all.

"All right," I replied before I changed my mind and started to hate myself for letting down the sisterhood, and hurting another woman to boot. This whole thing came down to a battle between good and evil. Honouring the sisterhood was good; having raging hormones, which fluctuated every millisecond toward a downhill slide into menopause, was evil.

The hormones won. And I found myself asking Monica, "So what happens next?" Whatever it was, and even though I felt lower than pond scum for what I was about to do, I fervently hoped I wouldn't come to regret it.

CHAPTER 2

On the flight back to Taipei that evening, I thought about my visit with Monica and how lucky I was to have her as a friend. She was the only person who could help in the strange situation in which I found myself, and I trusted her completely. I had always idolised her, and deep down I acknowledged that if I were more like Monica, I wouldn't feel quite so inadequate when it came to relationships or to life in general for that matter. Since my teens, I had lacked confidence in certain areas of my life, and over time Monica had become a crutch to support my sometimes flagging self-esteem.

Monica and I had known each other since our university days in London. From that time, which seemed so long ago now, she always managed to come to the rescue whenever I had relationship problems. She was the one who picked up and helped put together the thousands of pieces of my broken heart when the love of my life developed cold feet and called off our engagement—only to marry his secretary a few months later. *So much for the love of my life and his cold feet!*

After that traumatic experience, Monica had gone on to see me through many disastrous years of dates with commitment-phobic men who were only interested in one night stands—definitely not my scene. In the end, she even agreed with me that my vibrator made a better partner during the barren years. I knew she would have handled things differently if this had been the case with her own love life, which of course was always a varied and busy one.

Monica had never judged me or my choices. She simply let me be, the way any good friend would have done. Despite her support, however, the passage of time caught up with me and became my enemy. Each year that went by without a promising relationship became a year closer to the end of my childbearing age. By this time, I was in my late thirties and inevitably found myself thinking thus: If I meet a man by age thirty-nine, it will take at least one year for me to find out whether he's commitment-phobic, and at the same time rule out the possibility of his being a sex pervert, a pedophile, an axe murderer or something worse. By then, I'd be turning forty and, with any luck, we might just start thinking about living together. Another year will go by while we are getting used to living with each other, and suddenly I'm forty-one. Then, let's assume the man's more understanding than the Dalai Lama and can see the urgency of my situation—namely, that of wanting to start a family—and he sweeps me off my feet and marries me so we don't end up having a bastard child. After this, we spend another year trying to get me pregnant. After all, the chances of conceiving and carrying a child to term after age thirty-five drops by about sixty-five percent. By this time, I'm forty-two. Yikes!

Finally, God decides to grant me another miracle—yes, another one! The man being more understanding than the Dalai Lama was the first miracle—and now I fall pregnant. Nine months go by. I'm forty-three and heading into perimenopause by the time my child arrives. By then, I'll be having hot flashes and chronic backache—very common in women entering their menopausal years. So every time I bend down to pick up my baby, I'm putting even more strain on this back of mine, only to live out the rest of my days with a walking stick.

Therefore, it was easy to understand why, by my late thirties, I'd given up on the idea of finding love altogether. Still, it was always nice to know that through all my disappointments, Monica had never abandoned me. She truly was my idol, and I really wanted to be like her, except for the smoking part. Unlike me, she was strong, courageous, and confident—all wonderful qualities I admired. In fact, I was amazed that no one had ever managed to whisk her off her feet and marry her. God knows she never had any problems attracting men who wanted a commitment. Monica was smart, however, and didn't give her heart as easily as I did. She made men work for it even though she was the one who ended up doing the dumping in the end. Yes, I should have been more like her—the "love 'em and leave 'em" type. Then, I could've watched gleefully while my vibrator gathered dust and became entangled in spider web.

Sadly, my problems didn't end with the scarcity of relationships. My lack of self-confidence had stopped me from making some of my dreams come true, namely in the world of work. I found myself thinking yet again of my dear friend and comparing myself to her because not only was Monica popular with the opposite sex, but she was also a dynamic career woman. Being the head of an investment bank in Hong Kong was her trophy after many years spent hard at work. This was something she was not prepared to throw away for any man, hence her desire to remain single.

When her company managed to get past her supermodel looks, they realised she had a sharp brain, coupled with strong business acumen, and her next transfer reflected the pinnacle of her achievement. Now, she lived the life of a successful expatriate with a gorgeous apartment, maid service, and a chauffeur thrown in. Not bad at the ripe young age of thirty-nine.

Of course, when I compared myself to my idol, my life didn't look quite so glamorous even though it turned out to be somewhat exciting, if you could call it that. I ended up meeting someone in my late thirties. However, all was not as it seemed, and now I was struggling in Taipei to grow a network of people involved in a multi-level marketing company, which manufactured nutritional products, just so I could be near him. Plus in contrast to Monica's lifestyle, I lived in a pokey one-bedroom flat on the top floor of a rickety building that was full of rats. Luckily, the neighbour's cat was doing a wonderful job of killing the little buggers.

Overall, I couldn't complain about my present situation. I travelled for business between the UK, Hong Kong and Taiwan, and lived the life of a free-spirited entrepreneur minus the income. Well, we can't all be perfect like Monica. I didn't have maid service, but the landlady's mother let herself into my flat every morning to water a bunch of herbs she kept on the rooftop terrace, and sometimes she wiped down my kitchen counter. Besides, who needs a chauffeur in busy Taipei? The subway was fast and efficient. *Well done, Sarah, and to think I achieved all of this by the ripe old age of forty.*

Let's be honest—if there's one thing to be said about ageing, it's that a person is young until they reach the last year of their fourth decade. Then, over the period of one day—their birthday—they

7

suddenly enter the age of decline. Well, perhaps I was exaggerating just a little, but to reach the big four-oh and still be single was definitely not what I had planned for my life. I glumly reminded myself that the years were now really catching up with me and I still wasn't in the "living together" phase with my perfect man. Life just wasn't fair!

Having always been an independent woman who wanted both family and career, I had made a promise to myself that by the time I reached thirty, not only would I be happily married and on my way to having a baby, but I'd be running my own business empire. Sadly, in the harsh reality of modern day society, life rarely turned out as one planned. So I ended up in the singles' world where internet dating was all the rage and casual sex was the norm for most people. Whatever happened to romance and true love? *He ran away with his secretary, that's what!* I frowned as I felt the pain of my disillusionment all over again—even after twelve years had elapsed. God, had it really been that long since I'd been in a real relationship?

Thankfully, at this precise moment, the plane hit a small air pocket and my thoughts came back to the present. I had been rescued from spiralling into total depression and told myself it was time to focus on positive things like the future and my love for Jeffrey.

He had promised he'd meet me at the airport, and my heart did a double somersault in anticipation while butterflies fluttered in my stomach. The captain announced we were commencing our descent into Taipei, and the excitement of seeing Jeffrey kept mounting even when I lined up with hundreds of people at the immigration counter in Chiang Kai-shek airport a short while later. The Taiwanese authorities were slow in processing the incoming travellers so I switched on my mobile to check for messages and while away the time. In reality, I was hoping Jeffrey would ring to see whether I had landed safely. No messages and no missed calls. *Drats!*

Once through immigration, I rushed to baggage claim and picked up my small suitcase, now packed with new clothes I had purchased in Hong Kong—clothes I couldn't afford, but a worthwhile buy if Jeffrey saw me in them. Passing through the arrivals gate, my heart thumped so violently I thought it was going to leap out of my chest any minute, making people wonder if I had a small animal hidden inside my coat.

8

A sea of Asian faces greeted me when the doors to the arrivals lounge slid open, and the noise of loudly spoken Mandarin was everywhere around me. I looked desperately through the crowd while friends and relatives greeted one another and struggled with their luggage trolleys, but I couldn't find that familiar face, smiling a welcome as it had in my imagination only minutes earlier. Surely, he was here to meet me.

My mobile decided to vibrate at that moment, making me jump. "Hello," I spoke into it with the sinking feeling that this was going to be news of an unpleasant nature, and sure enough, it was.

"It's me," Jeffrey's voice whispered at the other end of the line.

I knew he was calling from somebody's bathroom. I could hear the unmistakable echo, which sounded like he was inside a fish bowl. My heart sank to my feet.

"Where are you?" I failed miserably at keeping the disappointment out of my voice.

"Kaohsiung." Then, he explained sheepishly, "Moira had a few appointments she wanted me to go to, and I couldn't say no."

Kaohsiung was around five hours by bus from Taipei. This meant I wouldn't be seeing him tonight. So much for the sexy lingerie and clothes I'd purchased. "Why didn't you make up some excuse?" I felt annoyed, disappointed, and wanted to cry all at the same time. "You knew I was coming back tonight and looking forward to seeing you. It's been a long two weeks without you."

The sound of Jeffrey flushing the toilet greeted me in response, and suddenly he was speaking in Mandarin. Oh, God! This could only mean one thing. Moira must be standing outside the bathroom door, listening to his telephone conversation. "She's there, right? Listening!" I wanted to scream with frustration but kept tight control over my tone.

"Correct," Jeffrey replied in Mandarin.

At least, I knew enough of the language to understand this much. "So when are you coming back?" The tone in my voice was tinged with desperation, but there was no reply from the other end. Obviously, Moira was still hanging around, and suddenly I was left listening to dead silence. Jeffrey must've hung up on me.

I wanted to throw the mobile across the airport but was fearful I might hit someone on the head with it. Instead, I stuffed it into my coat pocket and found a seat to support my weakening legs. To my dismay, I felt tears running down my face so I quickly faked a sneezing fit and made a big show of blowing my nose into a hankie. It worked every time.

How could he do this to me? I asked myself, feeling distraught. He should've told Moira by now that it was over between them. He'd promised he was going to do it by the time I returned from Hong Kong. *Whatever happened to my wish that he'd turn out to be more understanding than the Dalai Lama?*

Jeffrey knew I didn't like the subterfuge and lies that went with our relationship. I had no real sympathy for Moira because she was manipulative and clingy, but I'd always prided myself on being honest as far as relationships went. The game I was now forced to play for Jeffrey's sake was taking its toll on me, and I felt more and more like a traitor to the sisterhood. Sometimes, I simply felt like giving up altogether. But I was forty years old, and this was my last chance at a family.

The mobile vibrated again, and I jumped, my nerves in shreds. God, I was heading for a major anxiety attack. "Yes!" I barked into the phone, for I knew it would be him, and the echo from the bathroom at the other end confirmed it.

"Me again." He no longer whispered. It was obvious Moira was out of earshot. "Look, I'm really sorry about this. It was a last minute thing. You know the business is important, and I couldn't put it off."

I was suddenly fed up with his excuses. "So why doesn't Moira do the appointments by herself?" The threat of tears was evident in my voice. "You always tell me you stay with her because it's all too complicated, and you've been with her for so long, and she's part of the business, blah, blah, blah," I rambled on carelessly. "Well, if she really is part of the business, as you constantly claim, why didn't she go to Kaohsiung on her own? She knew I was coming back today, right? I know she talks to my team members behind my back and tries to find out my movements. Why doesn't she stop doing this? If she knows we're involved, why haven't you told her it's over? It seems to me you're just playing games!"

Jeffrey ignored my tirade of questions and accusations, and I had to bite my tongue in order not to blow up and have a major fit.

"I'm back tomorrow," he said. "I'll come round in the afternoon and we'll talk then; I promise. You know I want to see you, and I've missed you." His sweet voice had the tranquilising effect of a ten-milligram tablet of Valium, and suddenly I knew everything would be all right. Jeffrey still loved me, my heart sang. He missed me. He wanted me.

"Okay," I replied softly. "I'll see you tomorrow. I love you."

"Until tomorrow." He rang off.

***

Jeffrey was running late, which was nothing new. He was always late; and though I pointed this out to him repeatedly, he simply shrugged his shoulders and inevitably replied, "Business comes first."

It was a cold afternoon in Taipei and I waited in my room, wearing one of the sexy teddies I had purchased. It was a red slinky satin thing that accentuated the curves of my body, though it was a bit summery for the cooling weather. Still, I wanted to look just right for him.

I checked my appearance in the full length mirror of the sparsely furnished Japanese-style bedroom for what seemed to be the twentieth time or perhaps, it was the twenty-first—but who was counting? I was happy to note that the multitude of vitamins I consumed every day were really doing their job. I didn't look a day over thirty. Combined with the fact that I possessed a petite feminine figure and generous breasts, I was pleased to see that, although I wasn't the supermodel type like Monica, I was doing pretty well in the looks department, despite my pixie-like demeanour. Most importantly, my breasts hadn't even begun to re-route south as they usually did at this time in a woman's life.

A buzzing sound broke through my self-contemplation and I flew to the security intercom. "Yes?" I queried as if I wasn't expecting any visitors.

"It's me," Jeffrey's voice came over the line.

I buzzed him up and ran to the front door to wait for him. A few minutes later, we were back in my room, embracing passionately as we fell onto the bed, a rather hard Japanese futon, but I thought fleetingly that this wasn't the time to care about such things. I had my heart's desire, at least for now.

"You look delicious," Jeffrey whispered while he nibbled at my neck and squeezed one of my breasts with his hand.

Oh, yesssss! I felt wild currents of excitement course through my

11

body in anticipation of what was about to happen, and for a moment the thought crossed my mind that the scheme with Monica didn't seem to be so crazy after all. I just had to get Jeffrey away from Moira so he and I could finally be together, and…

Brrrr brrrr. Jeffrey's mobile started to ring.

"Leave it," I whispered through a haze of mounting passion, all other thoughts forgotten while he explored my body with smooth fingers.

Brrrr brrrr. The evil little noise continued to intrude through his erotic touch, but despite this I felt the tension in my body start to build toward "the magic moment".

Brrrr brrrr. *No! Oh, no!* Oh, God, he was going to answer it. Please, please don't! My brain cried desperately as my body arched with pleasure over the delicious sensation of his body against mine. And just when I was going to reach that wonderful, sublime moment I'd missed for so long, Jeffrey stopped cold and with one swift movement rolled away from me, swept up the ringing phone, and barked "hello" into it.

What followed was a tirade of unintelligible Mandarin, and I buried my head under a pillow in order to stop myself from screaming out in rage while Jeffrey spoke with Moira. Oh, yes, I knew it was Moira. Who else had the ability to detect a clandestine meeting with such accuracy? The woman was psychic when it came to knowing what Jeffrey was up to.

The tone in the conversation slowed down to a normal pace, and I sneaked a look at him. I wondered if he was trying to pacify her and let her down gently. Poor Jeffrey. He was probably trying to break it off with her, and though the length of time this was taking frustrated me to no end, I consoled myself with the thought that the man I loved was not a complete bastard. Any other guy would've dumped the woman a long time ago.

With Jeffrey still on the phone, my mind wandered. I suddenly wished I'd taken the time to learn Mandarin so I could figure out what in the blazes he was saying. It had taken him five years to master the language fully, and this was because he'd moved to Singapore as a teenager to join his parents, who were working there at the time. Though Jeffrey lived among the expat community, he nevertheless made many local friends, which accounted for his command of the language and how he'd met Moira, a "Singapore

Girl", as they used to say in the airline commercial.

A "Singapore Hag" was more like it, I thought venomously, seeing she was almost ten years his senior. Well, perhaps only eight. Of course, it didn't really matter that she was beautiful and petite. What mattered was that as an older woman, she had taken advantage of the shy young man Jeffrey used to be. And when she finally had him in her clutches, wham! She snapped the trap shut, and it had stayed shut despite the disintegration of their relationship over the years.

Everybody knew some Asian women put up with the infidelity of their men as long as they remained in a position of power, namely that of Wife Number One. Except that in Moira's case, Jeffrey didn't end up marrying her, so she was really classified as de-facto Wife Number One, now living with him as if she were his sister.

There was no longer anything physical in their relationship, and there hadn't been for years, but much to my chagrin, she still wielded immense power over him, and the trap remained firmly in place. The thought made me grind my teeth in frustration and anger.

After what seemed an interminable length of time, Jeffrey finally came off the phone and regarded me with his baby blues. "That was Moira." He sighed and leaned back on the bed, looking exhausted.

"I kind of gathered that." I failed to keep the sarcasm out of my voice. "So what's wrong with her this time? Is she lying on the side of the road, bleeding to death or committing hara-kiri for the tenth time?" *Oops!* The baby blues flashed a warning at me. "Okay, okay. I can't help it," I protested. "But don't you think these fake suicide attempts of hers are a bit much?"

Another look from those piercing eyes, and I stopped talking. What was the point of bringing up a repeatedly painful subject when he wasn't ready to make changes yet? I would just have to be patient a little longer and pray like crazy this Mike fellow could help me out. I was sure if Moira latched onto another man, she wouldn't find it quite so painful to let go of Jeffrey.

"So how was your trip?" Jeffrey rolled onto his side and drew me to him.

Mm! The last thing I wanted to talk about was business. "Productive," I whispered seductively against his mouth. I started to wrap my leg around his in order to bring him closer to me when his mobile rang once again.

Yes, it was Moira. This time, she wanted Jeffrey to come home because she had suddenly developed abdominal pains and was convinced she had to be hospitalised. I could have reminded him she had used the same excuse on the day before I left for my trip; but Jeffrey was already up, adjusting his clothes back in place while I foolishly admired his slim athletic body and wished he didn't have to go.

"I'll take her to the doctor and come back later," he said by way of apology.

"Don't bother. I don't think I could handle her committing suicide tonight." *Oops, again.* There was definitely acid dripping from my voice, but I didn't care.

Jeffrey ignored my comment and checked his appearance in the mirror. He seemed satisfied at the absence of telltale marks, and even his shiny black hair was magically in place.

It was at times like this I wished I was a smoker like Monica. Then, I could throw an ashtray at his head in the hope it would unscramble his brain and spur him into action so he could free himself of the ball and chain. Unfortunately, all I could do was throw evil looks his way, which did not stop him from making a hasty departure.

The moment he left, I rushed to the phone and dialled my good friend in Hong Kong. It was time to work out a strategy.

CHAPTER 3

The monthly cocktail function for Taipei's expat community was in full swing when I arrived at the luxurious Far Eastern Hotel. Normally, I hated going to these dos where everyone tried to outshine or outtalk one another. This was a tight knit group, and to sparkle was to be considered a success. It really didn't matter how full of crap you were as long as you were popular.

I cringed at the thought of having to make small talk with some fat Frenchman, reeking of smoke, or a half-drunk, middle-aged Aussie, trying to make a grab for my boobs. Unfortunately, this was where Monica had arranged for me to meet the formidable Mike, the man who would supposedly rescue me by sweeping Moira off her feet.

Moira! Just the thought of her gave me the creeps. For the last three weeks, since my return from Hong Kong, she had stalked me by calling constantly on the mobile every time I was with Jeffrey or by turning up at appointments we were attending together and pretending it was a big coincidence we'd bumped into each other. Then, Jeffrey was forced to let her hang out with us. After all, she was part of the business and had every right to be there, as he put it.

Grrr! The woman was impossible and relentless in her pursuit of Jeffrey. Talk about flogging a dead horse. Didn't she get it? He wasn't running after her anymore. Their relationship was over! *Grrr.*

"If you keep grinding your teeth like that, you're going to get a headache." A deep, smooth male voice cut through my image of Moira beating Jeffrey with a horsewhip. I looked up to meet a pair of sea-green eyes regarding me with amusement.

"Do you mind," I said, annoyed. "I'm waiting for someone."

"I know," replied the overconfident stranger. Perhaps, smug was a better description, I thought. *Grrrr.*

"You're doing it again," he remarked.

"What? What am I doing exactly?" For some reason, I found myself lashing out at this ... *mmmm* ... completely and devastatingly good looking man I didn't even know. Even through my mounting anger, I couldn't help but appreciate the fact that he was absolutely gorgeous in a typical Harlequin-hero sort of way—tall, dark, handsome, a strong jaw, and a shock of brown hair falling over those very startling green eyes ... *mmmm.*

Oh my! What the hell am I doing, drooling like a fool? I snapped out of my trance-like state, assuring myself the fluttering heart and the sudden weakening of my treacherous limbs had to do with Jeffrey rather than the complete stranger standing before me.

I didn't like these conflicting thoughts popping into my head, so I ignored them. I realised I'd been staring, but this didn't seem to faze the breathtaking vision before me and I almost dropped my wine glass at the sight of his sexy smile.

"You must be Sarah Jamison," Mr Romance stated, shaking my limp hand. "I'm Mike Connor, Monica's friend."

Well, knock me over with a feather! Monica certainly hadn't been exaggerating when she said women fell all over this guy. No wonder he was smug. So what was I doing, standing here like a speechless debutante?

"Oh," I managed to say as I buried my face in the wine glass, only to swallow the wrong way, breaking into a coughing fit that brought tears to my eyes. Mike grabbed my arm and pulled me away from the throng of onlookers.

Yes, they were all looking at me—even the half-drunk, middle-aged Aussie, whom I'm sure would've tried to make a grab for my boobs given half the chance.

Without knowing how it happened, I found myself seated in a quiet corner of the bar with a glass of cold water pressed into my hand. "Take a few sips," Mike instructed. "It'll make you feel better."

Like a good girl, I did as told and to my relief found the cool water did the trick. A handkerchief was thrust at me. "For the tears." Mike tried to keep the laughter out of his voice, and instead of becoming annoyed, I found myself laughing with him.

"I'm sorry." To my relief, I almost sounded normal again. "Thanks for this," I said, handing back the handkerchief.

"Can I get you another drink?" he offered, noticing my glass was empty.

"I'll have a cognac, thank you." I needed fortification to deal with the devastating Mike. Meanwhile, he merely raised a finger and a young waitress literally ran to him through the crowd to take the drinks order. Yes, the man had charm. Dangerous charm.

Mike turned to me once the order was placed and the waitress had reluctantly walked away. "So, I hope you are Sarah Jamison after all."

I smiled nervously. "Yes. Yes, I am." I was suddenly conscious of the silky black top I was wearing, which showed off my slim figure to its best advantage.

"Monica told me you had a project I couldn't refuse, so I said I'd meet you to find out all about it."

This time, I spat out the water in my mouth and saturated the front of my blouse. "You mean ..." No, it couldn't be! "You mean ..." I tried again. "You mean Monica didn't give you the details?"

"That's right," Mike replied with his devastating smile, totally unaware of the chaos he was causing while I dabbed madly at my chest with a paper napkin, trying frantically to keep a cool head. "She just said I would find it difficult to resist. And being a stranger to Taipei, I thought it an excellent opportunity to make new contacts. Are you in investment banking?"

OH, MY GOD! I'll kill you, Monica! I screamed in silent rage while I kept wiping at my blouse. How could she do this to me? She'd told me not to worry about a thing, that she would set everything up; and this was her idea of setting things up? This was typical Monica with her sick sense of humour. She was trying to set me up with Mike, the-wonderful-femme-fatale-only-he-was-male. After all, she'd told me to forget Jeffrey. "He's bad news," she'd said. "Why are you waiting for somebody who doesn't want to be free?"

"What do you mean?" I'd asked her while my heart broke to bits.

"He's got the best of both worlds: you in one corner, all sexy and ready to romp, and Moira in the other, the mother figure and his security blanket."

Monica could be brutally honest at times, and that had been one of them. So when she'd suggested Mike for the job, it was obvious she'd had no intention of his charming Moira off her feet. All along, she'd been secretly matchmaking me with the man. I fumed as I finally accepted the fact that the cigarettes had definitely taken their toll on her brain and she had truly lost her mind.

"Sarah, are you okay?" Mike sounded concerned. "Your face is flushed. Would you like to get out of here? It's rather hot in this place."

"No. No, it's okay, really," I reassured him, drinking more water to buy some time and try to calm myself. I had to think fast about how I was going to get out of this one. I really couldn't tell him the truth. He'd think me childish and stupid. In fact, the whole scheme was stupid, and I didn't know why I'd ever thought of it in the first place.

The waitress arrived with our drinks and this gave me a few more precious moments in which to think. I would have to tell him there had been some sort of mistake; possibly, that Monica misunderstood the whole situation and thought I had a great contact for him, though it fell through. Just tell him anything other than the truth.

Rule number one: when in trouble, lie. So, just as I was about to open my mouth to deliver one of my better lies, I was shocked into total silence when my eyes fixed on the two people suddenly standing before our table.

"Hello there! What a coincidence running into you," exclaimed a familiar, high-pitched voice that grated on my nerves.

I immediately pasted a smile on my face. "Moira, how are you? And Jeffrey." *If looks could kill!*

Mike was on his feet in an instant, shaking Jeffrey's hand and settling Moira into a seat. "Hello, I'm Mike Connor. Just got in from Hong Kong and getting to know the local population." He motioned for the eager waitress and asked what the others wanted to drink.

This gave me time to throw a furious look at Jeffrey, but he had the good sense to avoid my eyes; otherwise, he would've seen the murderous intent in them. Moira, on the other hand, seemed to be absolutely entranced with Mike. My frazzled brain did an about-face and suddenly I knew my stupid scheme wasn't so stupid after all. It was brilliant. It would work. All I had to do now was tell Mike the truth—well, as soon as was practicably possible.

Jeffrey made the introductions. "I'm Jeffrey Williams, and this is my girlfriend, Moira Sun."

I searched for an ashtray to throw at his head, but sadly we were in a non-smoking area. Girlfriend, indeed! Why not introduce her as his mother-figure-security-blanket-totally-paranoid-with-suicidal-tendencies-ball-and-chain? I fumed inwardly.

"Sun as in sunshine?" Mike asked, treating Moira to one of his sexy smiles. I tried to keep myself from being sick.

Moira was all giggles. "You are so kind."

"Not at all. Praise is always due where beauty's present," Mike replied.

Oh, puhleeese! I rolled my eyes and took a big swig of cognac.

Jeffrey seemed unconcerned at Mike's flirty remark. "So, Mike, what is it that you do?"

"I'm in investment banking; and Sarah was kind enough to come up with a wonderful project for me." His eyes shot a look in my direction and if I was not mistaken, there was mischief written all over them—he knew something underhand was going on inside my head. Of course he knew! He wasn't born yesterday. My face must've gone bright red because it suddenly felt like I was on fire. I knew I was in real trouble.

Jeffrey saw my discomfort, but his interest got the better of him. "Really, and what project is that?"

Mike grinned in my direction and waited for me to reply.

It was at this moment that I realised I hated men, no matter how good looking they were. All men were bastards, and bastards always hung out with other bastards. Let's face it, Jeffrey was a bastard, cheating on paranoid Moira and keeping me at a distance; and Mike was a smug bastard, who should have been born in the Middle East so he could keep a harem.

The cognac hit the spot nicely and I was finally able to face them with dignity and rule number one firmly imprinted in my brain. "It's just someone I met not long ago who's in investment banking over here. I thought Mike should meet him seeing as he's new to Taipei and all that." Another swig of cognac and I was totally in my element. Well, almost.

"I didn't know you knew people in investment banking," Jeffrey remarked with curiosity.

"Well," and this time it was I who was smug, "you don't need to know everything, Jeffrey." Big smile. That took care of him and his one thousand and one questions.

Meanwhile, Mike was smirking behind his drink, and Moira looked rather confused and, for once, had nothing to say. Luckily, my mobile rang and I was saved from further explanation. "Excuse me," I said and walked off to take the call. I reached the ladies' toilet before I hit the answer button. "Thanks a lot, Monica!"

"How did you know it was me? Caller ID doesn't show on overseas calls."

"Who else is going to call around the time I'm supposed to be meeting Mr Wonderful?" It was a shame Monica was all the way in Hong Kong, I thought; otherwise, my fingers would be wrapping themselves around her neck right about now.

"Are you very mad at me?" Monica had a way of sounding like a little girl when all else failed.

"Mad isn't even close," I replied, "but I forgive you." Magnanimously, I added, "I know you meant well."

"Really?" She sounded truly surprised and then a little suspicious. "What's going on?"

"Things turned out for the best after all," I explained. "Jeffrey and Moira made a coincidental appearance, and she went all goggle-eyed when she met Mike." I couldn't help the glee in my voice.

"Oh."

"You sound disappointed," I remarked. "And if you were trying to fix me up with Mr Green Eyes, you failed miserably. I mean, the guy really loves himself."

"That's not true," Monica protested on Mike's behalf. "You don't know him. Deep down inside, he's a really nice guy."

With sarcasm dripping from my voice, I replied, "You mean there's a deep down? Frankly, I thought he was all superficiality."

"Since when are you an authority on first impressions?" Monica sounded annoyed.

"Since I met Mike Connor," I returned tartly.

"Fine! Think what you like, but Mike is a lot more decent than Jeffrey. At least, he doesn't cheat on his women." Monica persisted in standing up for the guy.

"That's probably because he hasn't been with one long enough," I said smugly.

"You're impossible sometimes, Sarah. Go ahead with your plan, and if you really end up with Jeffrey, don't ask me to feel sorry for you later." Monica seemed really upset, and suddenly I felt guilty. Her heart was in the right place and she *was* my best friend.

"Look, I'm sorry. Really, I am," I sighed into the phone. "I've just had a very taxing evening and the alcohol's making me say things I don't mean."

"All right, don't worry. Go home and rest. If you do decide to tell Mike about the scheme, believe me, he will help you. He's that kind of guy."

"I'll call you tomorrow." I wished her good night and rang off as I caught my image in the mirror. I looked like a normal person again and pleased to see I was no longer flushing. I flicked a stray strand of hair off my face and went back out.

"Where are they?" I asked Mike when I returned to the table and found him alone.

"They had an appointment to go to."

I sat down, prepared to finally tell him the truth, when he put up a hand to stop me from talking. "You're in love with that guy and you want me to charm his girlfriend away from him, right?" My mouth must have dropped wide open. "I see you're no longer grinding your teeth," he added with a gleam in his eye.

He was such a smartarse, but I had no time to reflect on his bad qualities right now. "How did you know?" I uttered, totally dumbfounded.

"God, Sarah, it was obvious by the way you were looking at him," he remarked.

Could it be Mike Connor was intuitive underneath his veneer of egotistical vanity? I searched his face for a moment and instead of seeing the sneer I had expected there, I saw a flash of kindness; but it quickly disappeared, replaced by the gleam.

"You're right," I plunged into the truth with relief. "You're absolutely right."

"So tell me all," he urged.

I was surprised he even wanted to know. I thought he would have laughed and made a snide remark of some sort; but instead he seemed genuinely interested in listening to what I had to say. So I told him. I gave him the background on Jeffrey and his platonic relationship with Moira, including his inability to make "the break" due partly to Moira's manipulative ways and to his feelings of guilt. I then felt astonished when I confessed my undying love for Jeffrey and my dream that soon he would be free to be with me.

"I've been involved with him for just over a year and I'm not about to give up now." I avoided looking into Mike's eyes when I finished speaking, peering into my cognac instead.

"And this guy loves you back?" Mike went straight to the heart of the matter.

"Yes," I replied, although my voice did not seem to echo my strong conviction, and I fleetingly wondered whether he sensed this.

Mike made no judgement. He gazed pensively at me while he finished his drink. "Okay," he said finally, "I'll help you."

"You will?" I was astounded at how quickly he made his decision. Perhaps, the guy was not as bad as I'd thought.

"There is one condition, however," Mike added.

There I go again, always jumping to conclusions straight away. Of course the guy was bad! After all, who would agree to romance a strange woman, only to dump her once he was through with her? A lot of very sick guys, that's who. Guys like Mike Connor. "What's the condition?" I reluctantly asked, ignoring my thoughts and the guilt I felt at setting up Moira for a fall.

"We play this both ways," Mike explained. "I charm Moira away from Jeffrey, and you make Jeffrey jealous."

"Jealous? Why would I need to make him jealous?" I asked, puzzled.

"Don't you know anything about men, Sarah?"

Even if I didn't, I certainly wasn't going to admit it to Mr High-and-Mighty. And to think moments earlier I'd thought he wasn't half bad. "What are you talking about?" I felt affronted.

"Men don't want to have it handed to them on a silver platter, you know. They still like the hunt; so let him fight for you." He threw me a confident smile.

Of all the conceited, arrogant, condescending things to say! "Listen, Mike, I don't know what kind of women you're used to, but I love Jeffrey; and I'm not about to play silly 'come and get me' games with him. So let's stick to doing this my way, which is to charm Moira." The man was insufferable and I wanted to wipe that amused glint from his eyes, but I was rapidly running out of imaginary ashtrays.

"Okay," he agreed readily, too readily. This aroused my suspicion. "What now?" he asked, noticing the look I gave him.

"Nothing," I remarked innocently. I would have to keep an eye on Mike Connor until I found out if he could be trusted. What if he went and told Moira about the scheme? The doubt reared its ugly head and I couldn't put it completely from my mind.

"We need to draw up a plan of action," Mike stated, ignoring the flitting expressions I was sure must have been crossing my face.

"Yes, a plan of action," I repeated and paid attention.

"It can't be too obvious that I'm after her," he explained. "I'm going to need your help with her schedule so I can arrange to bump into her and take it from there."

"Okay," I agreed. *This shouldn't be too hard.*

"Fine," he nodded resolutely. "Give me a call when you have the information."

I took this as a hint that the evening was over and he was eager to go home. "Here's my business card," I said, fishing one out of my bag and handing it to him.

Mike wrote out his number on a paper napkin. "Sorry, I'm still waiting for mine."

I reached for the napkin and stuffed it in my bag as I stood up. "I'll be in touch then," my tone was businesslike, and I shook his hand.

Mike regarded me with what I now thought of as his "glint of amusement" and I pursed my lips to stop myself from saying something I would later regret. The guy had just agreed to help me out and I couldn't afford to give offence—unfortunately.

"Good night." He smiled knowingly as if he could read my thoughts. "It was very refreshing meeting you—again."

And what was that supposed to mean? "Good night," I replied and left the bar with the feel of those sea-green eyes burning into my back. Only then did I realise, much to my mortification, that I was supposed to have met him at Monica's Christmas party and due to the amount of alcohol I had consumed at the time, I didn't remember him at all. What must he think of me? *Well, I don't care.* I hurried out of the hotel, my thoughts in turmoil.

CHAPTER 4

As soon as I returned from the cocktail party, I was on the phone to my mother in London. "Just run a search on him, Mum. *Mike Connor* or try *Michael* if you can't find anything under Mike," I spoke through clenched teeth, thinking about the trouble I was putting myself through because of Moira, the ball and chain.

"Are you grinding your teeth, dear? You'll get a headache, you know," my mother admonished me.

Why was everyone telling me this? "Mum!"

"All right, dear," my mother said, "but why do you want to run a background check on this man? What are you up to, Sarah? I hope you're not in some kind of trouble."

The questions kept coming thick and fast, and I gave her a watered-down version of my scheme to get Jeffrey.

"But, dear," my mother exclaimed, sounding puzzled, "why do you have to go to this extent just to get a man? I thought you said Jeffrey was in love with you and that the two of you were happy together."

I winced at the white lie I had told her when I'd first become involved with Jeffrey. We were definitely not "together"; at least, not yet. "Of course we're in love, Mum! But it's a little more complicated than that," I tried to remain patient as I spoke. The last thing I needed was to have an argument with her over the phone.

My mother was not going to let me off the hook so easily, however. "I don't see what can be so complicated, Sarah. He either loves you or he doesn't," she stated in the logical manner that older and wiser people possessed, especially when they were on the outside looking in.

I sighed while I tried to control my temper. "Never mind this now. Can't you just run the search for me?"

"Of course, I'll do it, dear, if that's what you want. But I just don't understand you young people, hiring some man to steal away the woman of the man you love. Why would anybody do that, I ask you? And how much are you paying this Lothario?"

Oh, God, a Lothario. Surely, we'd stopped using words like this in the 21st century. "What are you talking about?"

"Really, Sarah," replied my mother, annoyed, "you can be so obtuse at times."

Where did she come up with all these words? Obtuse. Lothario. What next?

"This man sounds like a gigolo," my mother went on.

Okay, at least this was a more fashionable way of putting it. "He's not a gigolo, and I'm not paying him anything," I stated truthfully.

"Are you sleeping with him, then?"

"Mother!"

"Don't 'Mother' me, dear," she admonished. "I'm not totally wet behind the ears, you know. Just because your father was the only man in my life, it doesn't mean I didn't have my flirts before I met him. Of course, in those days, it was all quite innocent. Now, people jump into bed with anybody at the drop of a hat. It's really disgusting what this generation has come to, and I think—"

"Mum!" I cut in rather rudely. "We're talking long distance, remember?" At this rate, my phone call was going to cost me a week's rent.

"Okay, okay. So you want me to run a search on this man, Mike Connor," my mother repeated yet again.

"Yes!" I snapped, impatience getting the better of me.

"Well, give me the details of where he works, dear. The net's very efficient these days, but I like to have something to give me a start." She was all business now.

I rolled my eyes in exasperation and gave her Mike's details. I couldn't help but think how bizarre this whole thing was. Here was my mother at age seventy with her old-fashioned ways, becoming an internet junkie and developing a select network of women from various parts of the world who formed an investigations club over the net.

My mother was the creator and administrator of a website called *Cat's Eye*, and she and her friends ran a snooping business. If it was on the net, they found it; if it wasn't, they hacked into where they could find it.

My mother went by the net identity of Rosepurple, and her reputation was well known, or so I had been told by several of my UK friends who had utilised her services for various purposes. Generally, her group ran background checks on people; they could find out almost anything: where they were born, education history, career moves, their credit background, criminal record, whether they purchased sex toys over the net, and the list went on.

It was amazing how most things people thought private were actually on a server somewhere, waiting to be found by some hacker like my mother. Not only this, but the fact that she was making more money than I by running this business was a real blow to my pride, even though it was admirable. What was more than admirable, however, was that anyone who came across *Cat's Eye* without a referral thought this was a group of women dedicated to designing and exchanging e-cards featuring cats and kittens. This was their cover, and it was working extremely well because absolutely no one from any privacy committee or government agency had caught up with them to date.

I was a little frightened at what might happen to my mother if they ever did. Knowing her, though, she would probably spoof her way to some untraceable destination like Upper Mongolia where even the CIA would be given the runaround.

"Okay, dear, consider this one a freebie," my mother's voice broke into my thoughts. "I'll email you the results."

"Thanks, Mum." I couldn't keep the sarcasm out of my voice.

"Just kidding, Sarah." My mother rang off.

She always had the last word, and somehow I felt like I'd been reprimanded. Of course, she wouldn't charge me for her services, but these days I wasn't so sure anymore. The whole thing was just too surreal.

Rosepurple, as I chose to think of her, had changed significantly since my dad passed on two years before. While he'd been alive, she had been a stable and supportive housewife. As soon as she was widowed and turned to the internet for comfort, a new person emerged—a hardheaded businesswoman who hacked her way to success.

Having grown up with a fussing and caring mother figure, it came as a big shock that I was suddenly related to a snoop called Rosepurple. Still, like all things in life, this, too, had a reason for happening; and who better than my very own mother to give me the real lowdown on the priceless Mr Connor?

I had asked for a search on everything Rosepurple could get her hands on, even right down to where Mike purchased his underwear. I was determined to find out all I could about Mr Know-it-all in case he double-crossed me. Besides, I mused, it didn't hurt to have ammunition in matters like this. In such situations, information was power, and I was going to ensure Mr Connor did not get the upper hand.

CHAPTER 5

Things sounded too good to be true, I thought while I listened to Mike over lunch at a café near his office.

"... and she sat next to me through the whole seminar and even invited me to lunch afterwards," he finished recounting his story.

I had arranged for him to attend a nutrition seminar hosted by my company's head office, one I knew Moira would be attending. What was surprising was that Jeffrey had also been present, having cancelled a business trip at the last minute.

"Are you listening, Sarah?" Mike's voice intruded in on my wandering thoughts.

"Yes, of course." I couldn't understand it, but something told me things were not quite right. I turned my serious gaze on Mike. "So Jeffrey was there, but Moira sat next to you?" I queried, all the while trying to digest the details he had so far divulged.

"That's what I just said, if you were listening." He sounded irritated, and I wondered whether it bothered him that a female's attention was on another man instead of on him. It was obvious his ego wasn't used to this kind of treatment, and I couldn't help but smile at the thought. Poor Mike.

"What's the smile for?" he almost barked.

Oh, he's deliciously annoyed. Good. I chose to ignore his question. "Okay, so she sat next to you, with Jeffrey in the same room," I repeated thoughtfully as I watched him take a gulp of hot coffee, which I thought he might end up spitting in my face.

"Yes!" he snapped.

I remained impervious to his obvious impatience. "And then she asked you to lunch. Alone." This, I couldn't believe, but Mike insisted it was the truth.

"So where was Jeffrey all this time?" I couldn't stand the suspense any longer.

"How the hell should I know? I didn't keep tabs on him!" Mike spat out.

The man was definitely upset, and I couldn't believe he had such a fragile ego. Served him right for being so sure of himself all the time. Moira may fall all over him, but Mr Connor wasn't making a single dent on me. At least, not if I can help it, I thought involuntarily. What was the matter with me, anyway? I didn't even get to find out what Jeffrey thought when Mike and Moira went off to lunch; and here I was, wasting time and mooning about Mike and my possible attraction to him. God, the man was insufferable!

"Is something wrong?" I asked when I noticed the object of my thoughts glaring my way.

"No, but if you've had enough details for today, I'd like to get back to work."

It suddenly dawned on me that I may have misjudged him, and he wasn't annoyed because of his ego. Maybe, he's already fed up with the project! I panicked. I couldn't afford to have him quit on me now, not when things were beginning to work out. Somehow, I must've insulted the great Mike, and I had to make amends immediately.

"I'm so sorry. I didn't realise you had a busy schedule today," I apologised as sincerely as I could. "Thank you for doing this. I really appreciate it."

"Yes, well ..." He went to reach for the bill, but I beat him to it.

"Lunch is on me," I said and saw a frown on his face. *What's wrong now?*

"Thanks for lunch, then. But I really have to go now," he uttered abruptly and before I could reply, he faded into the lunchtime crowd without so much as a wave goodbye.

I couldn't figure out what his problem was, and I didn't even want to try. Perhaps, he was one of those guys who didn't like the woman to pay on a date. But we hadn't been out on a date. This was work, I reminded myself while I pulled out a piece of paper from my handbag. It was a copy I'd made of the email Rosepurple sent me earlier that morning.

Mike's background check had come up squeaky clean—not even a purchase of kinky underwear, much to my disappointment. I had nothing on the man! And judging from his behaviour over lunch, he was probably regretting his decision to help me. So I didn't think I would be needing any ammunition against him, which was just as well. Besides, from what I'd observed so far, Mike Connor struck me as someone who kept his word, and I doubted he would blab anything to Moira about our little project.

Thoughts of Mike were momentarily forgotten when I went back over the information I'd learned from him. Moira had gone to lunch with him, leaving Jeffrey behind. This was most unusual behaviour for her, but definitely a major step in the right direction. After all, she followed Jeffrey absolutely everywhere. Leaving him alone to go off with another man was unthinkable. Could it be really possible she was beginning to fall for Mike? The thought was so exciting that I called Jeffrey from my mobile.

"Have time for a visit?" I asked in my sexiest voice when he answered the call.

"I'll meet you at your place in half an hour," was the reply.

Yes! Things were definitely looking up. I paid the bill and hurried home.

***

"What was your friend doing at the seminar?" Jeffrey asked as soon as he arrived.

I was taken aback. "Why do you want to know?" I hoped like hell he hadn't caught on to my little scheme.

"Just wondering," he replied thoughtfully. "Moira seemed happy to see him."

My relief at not being found out was short-lived and my stomach plummeted to my feet. "And this bothers you?" I managed to sound casual. Surely, he wasn't jealous of Mike.

"Not particularly—only the fellow knows she's my girlfriend, and yet he goes out to lunch with her without asking me to join them."

I couldn't believe what I heard, and unfortunately lost my temper. "So what?" I exclaimed in anger. "I thought you said you didn't want to be with her anymore. You told me hundreds of times you wish she'd find another man and leave you. So what's the problem now?" I felt so upset I couldn't stand still; therefore, I paced the room while I fumed.

"Hey, what's come over you? Calm down." Jeffrey went to reach for me, but I evaded his arms and kept pacing.

"What is it with you?" I uttered, on the verge of tears. "Have you been lying to me all along? Perhaps, despite everything, you really want Moira to stay with you." Just as I said this, Monica's words came back to haunt me, and I didn't like the feeling one bit—*Why are you waiting for someone who doesn't want to be free?*

Had Monica been right all along? This was ridiculous, I argued with myself. Jeffrey loved me. He wanted to be with me. He said so all the time.

What makes you so sure, Sarah? This came from the little voice inside my head. I was about to burst into tears of frustration when a pair of arms came up from behind and pulled me against a hard chest. "Stop this," Jeffrey whispered in my ear. "You know I love you."

The tears disappeared and my distress turned to desire for him. Moira and Mike were temporarily forgotten as Jeffrey's fingers reached out to unbutton my blouse. *Yes, oh, yes. Baby, I'm home!*

After a rather long and passionate lovemaking session without any telephone interruptions, Jeffrey left to go back to work, and I sat around my small flat, thinking it was time to change my strategy. If Jeffrey had been annoyed about Moira developing a possible attraction for Mike, how much more annoyed would he be if it was I who suddenly developed an attraction for Mr Green Eyes?

Mike's idea of making Jeffrey jealous had merit, I now acknowledged, and there was no real harm in playing a little game of "come and get me" with him, as Mike had suggested. I smiled in anticipation. The only thing I needed to do was convince Mike to go along with it. Admittedly, the thought of having to confess he'd been right all along made me squirm. My smile turned into a frown. I was sure his ego was going to grow big enough to engulf the whole city of Taipei and beyond when I told him. Ugh! To think I would have to swallow my pride … But it was for a good cause. So, before I changed my mind, I telephoned him at his office.

"Yes." Mike's abrupt greeting was not a good beginning.

I winced. "Sorry to bother you, Mike. I know you're busy." God,

I could sound so meek when I wanted. "I just wondered if you'd like to attend a Chinese New Year's party with me." My stomach suddenly felt squeamish. I couldn't believe I was asking Mr Beautiful out on a date.

"Why?"

And he wasn't going to make it easy for me, either. "What do you mean 'why'?" I clenched my teeth to stop myself from raising my voice. "There's a party for New Year's and Moira's going to be there, so I—"

"I see," Mike interrupted. "For a moment, I thought you were asking me out because you genuinely wanted to see me."

Was he laughing at me? "Of all the conceited and arrogant … Look, just forget it, all right?" I hung up on him and visualised a whole bunch of ashtrays hurtling through the air toward his big, ego-inflated head.

The telephone rang. "What?" I answered harshly.

"Of course, I'd love to go with you," Mike said in a soft and sexy voice. "Don't get upset. I couldn't resist having a bit of fun."

Well, I thought with indignation, when he put it this way, I had no choice but to forgive him. Were all men such charming bastards or was it just my exclusive privilege to encounter them all?

CHAPTER 6

I took extra care with my appearance on the night of the party. In fact, I made sure I had a good night's sleep so I wouldn't get puffy eyes, my typical misfortune whenever I had a late night these days. I was now pleased to find that my hazel eyes sparkled and held a look of excitement I hadn't seen in them of late.

I stopped preening in front of the mirror. Mike, the wonder date, would be arriving shortly, and I was only halfway through my make-up. When I was ready, I stood back from the full-length mirror to survey the results.

The burnt-orange, silk cheongsam dress with gold piping around the collar and splits on either side of its long skirt, looked stunning and even matched the colour of my hair. I acknowledged on this occasion that I was pleased with my appearance and had nothing to criticise.

I wore my hair up, secured by carved, imitation ivory combs, and my feet were encased in the most delicate high-heeled gold sandals. To finish off the dramatic effect, I draped a gossamer-thin cream shawl around my shoulders. My eyes looked very large in my face, and I was suddenly reminded of my mother's cat, Mitzy. She was all eyes in a small delicate face. Of course, I didn't have the whiskers. I laughed at the comparison and almost jumped out of my skin when the security buzzer broke the silence in the flat. I spoke into it, knowing it could only be my date. "I'll be right down."

"Okay," was Mike's response.

One last look in the mirror and I picked up an envelope evening bag, the same colour as my sandals, and rushed out. While I tackled the endless stairs leading down to street level, I wondered whether I should have invited Mike into my place, but to my surprise I realised I didn't want him to see the squalid little unit where I lived. Heaven forbid the landlady's mother should take it into her head to choose that same exact moment to walk in and tend to her beloved herbs. But it was more than this—I simply didn't want Mike to see me surrounded by what I could only think of as scarcity. When it came to my lifestyle and business, I wanted him to think I was doing well.

When I reached the front door to my building, I stopped short for a moment. Mike looked absolutely breathtaking in a tux, which complemented his athletic form to perfection—move over, James Bond—and made his impossibly green eyes seem even greener. I told my treacherous heart to calm down as it skipped a few beats. *Remember, this is the enemy. A means to an end. Charming Bastard No 1.*

"Wow," Mike uttered, running a rather intimate glance up and down my body with an appreciative look.

I felt a searing flash of heat start from the roots of my hair and spread right down to my toes. I knew my body was probably not yet ready for the start of menopause, so the cause of this reaction was definitely not the change of life, but rather Mike's approving gaze.

"You look great," he added, not noticing anything unusual like the fact that I was probably as red as a tomato. Despite the heat surging through my treasonous body, I managed a smile and then noticed the chauffeur-driven Mercedes waiting for us.

"Hmm," I commented, trying not to sound too impressed. "We travel in style, I see."

"One of the perks of the job," Mike informed me in a matter-of-fact tone. "So let's go and confront the enemy." This was said in jest and with a grin that showed off perfect white teeth. I felt inexplicably annoyed all of a sudden. Why did he have to look so good?

I figured him to be somewhere in his early forties and was sure he would go on looking fantastic well into old age. It was always like this with charming bastards, I thought in irritation. They looked good at any age, and they knew it.

In my opinion, it was totally unacceptable that Mother Nature had committed such a ghastly mistake as to allow men to age gracefully. Furthermore, Mother Nature had no business making Mike Connor so difficult to resist.

Meanwhile, women had to worry about starting a family before it was too late; not to mention having to find the love of their life so they could start the family in the first place. Plus women had to look damn good while trying to achieve the impossible. This was obvious proof that Mother Nature was really a man. I hated Mother Nature or was it *Father* Nature?

The limo negotiated its way smoothly in the heavy Taipei traffic while I relaxed into the soft leather of the back seat. I shook off my thoughts and tried to ignore my palpitating heart. I was sure Mike had this effect on all women. Besides, I reminded myself, my true feelings were reserved for Jeffrey and not for my pretend date.

"So what's in store for you in the Year of the Rat?" Mike's question jolted me out of my musing.

Trust this to be the Year of the Rat. It may as well be called the Year of the Bastard. "Who knows," I returned flippantly, "but I could certainly use all the luck I can get."

I thought I caught a frown crossing his brow as if he was judging me. If so, he didn't give any indication of it when he asked, "Don't you think you'd better fill me in on the evening ahead? We're about ten minutes away from the hotel."

We were attending a big expat ball at the Far Eastern Hotel to welcome in the New Year, and one of my team members, who had connections with the regular expat crowd, managed to wrangle an invitation for me in the hope that I would work the floor with her. Tonight, however, I wasn't in the mood for networking the business. My only aim in going to the ball was purely to throw Mike in Moira's path. After his recent lunch with her, I believed my goal was well within my grasp, and nothing, not even a magnitude ten earthquake, was going to stand in my way.

"Hey, I'm waiting." Mike waved a hand in front of my face to attract my attention.

How this must gall him, I thought, smiling wickedly. Finally a female who wasn't hanging on his every word. Still, I couldn't afford to be rude, not since the man was doing me a huge favour. "I'm sorry." I gave him a dazzling smile and lied, "I was enjoying the passing scenery."

"Not as breathtaking as Hong Kong, but Taipei does have its charms," he replied, looking meaningfully at me.

I cleared my throat and hoped he wasn't getting any ideas. "Okay, here's the deal." I got down to business in a rather harsh voice, thinking this might distract him from whatever "charms" he was talking about. "Jeffrey and Moira will be networking their way around the crowd. This is what they always do at parties. They don't have fun; they simply network."

Just thinking about the number of times Jeffrey had cancelled on me because of "the business" succeeded in irritating me, and it occurred that I seemed to be increasingly irritable these days. I anxiously wondered if I was going into menopause after all. I shuddered at the thought and forced myself to ignore the horrible possibility. "Anyway," I went on, trying to focus on the conversation with Mike, "I want you to monopolise Moira's time as much as you can, even if you have to pretend an interest in the business."

"Are they as bad as all that?" Mike seemed genuinely curious. "I mean, I can relate to having to network for business, but it shouldn't take over one's entire life."

"You don't understand," I jumped to Jeffrey's defence, feeling even more irritated—this time at Mike's ignorance. "This is network marketing we're talking about, not some cushy expat job with a fat salary! We have to be on our toes at all times."

"Sorry if what I do offends you," he stated with a hint of sarcasm.

"Mike," I sighed, trying to control my already frayed nerves, "I'm only trying to give you an idea of how cut-throat our business is." I quelled my desire to hit him across the head and, at the same time, cursed myself for letting Mike, the Mega Ego, get to me.

Luckily, he ignored my remark and brought the conversation back to the topic at hand. "Okay, so I monopolise Moira's time as much as I can. And I suppose you want me to flirt outrageously with her, too?"

I didn't react to the cynicism in his tone. I was too preoccupied, thinking about my pending menopause and my plans for the evening. I hoped the evening, at least, turned out to be a success. Unfortunately, I couldn't do much about the cursed menopause. "Yes. Yes. Flirt. Be charming. Promise her the world, if you have to. I want Jeffrey to see she isn't as clingy as she makes out to be."

"You mean you want her to transfer her clinginess from Jeffrey to me," Mike remarked in the same cynical tone of voice.

I felt my temper rise. "Who cares who she clings to as long as it's not Jeffrey!"

36

Mike ignored my outburst. "And what about you, making Jeffrey jealous? Shouldn't I be paying some attention to you, too?"

He had a point. In my excitement about the evening, I had forgotten all about my agreement with his plan to make Jeffrey jealous. "Fine," I exclaimed. "Divide your time equally between us," and I added sarcastically, "I'm sure you won't have a problem doing that."

Mike didn't rise to the bait but threw me a look of concern instead. "I only hope this guy's worth all the trouble you're putting yourself through." His sobering words rendered me silent and we completed the rest of the journey without further conversation.

The ballroom at the Far Eastern Hotel glittered with all manner of Chinese lanterns and twinkling multi-coloured lights. It was a paradise of brightness, welcoming guests into its warmth. When Mike and I entered the room, we were immediately accosted by Ping, the Taiwanese team member who had invited me.

Ping was usually a shy person who said very little, which was why she always wanted me to help her talk to people about the business. The minute she saw Mike, however, she gave him a big goofy smile and launched into a tirade of greetings and general chatter that left me momentarily speechless. Was there anyone at all out there who was immune to the man's charm? Of course not. To top it all off, I reminded myself, this was his year, the Year of the Rat.

"Ping," I interrupted halfway through her torrent of words, "this is a friend of mine, Mike Connor. Mike, this is Ping Wang, one of the brighter stars in my team."

"So very nice to meet you, Mike." Ping squinted up at him through thick-framed glasses. "Have you been long in Taipei?"

Mike gave her one of his devastating smiles, much to my annoyance. At this rate, Ping was never going to leave us alone. "Only a few weeks. It's a charming city." For a moment, his gaze slid over me.

Here we go again! I fumed. If he mentioned the word *charming* one more time, I was going to hit him. "Ping," I jumped in before he said anything further, "isn't that Mark Lau over there? He seemed quite interested in the vitamin pack when I spoke with him last week, but he wanted someone to explain things to him in Chinese. Perhaps, you can help out."

Ping's squint turned to me. "Of course. I will go right now."

Turning back to Mike, she said, "So nice to meet you, Mike, and welcome. I will come back later to chat with you." She threw him another goofy smile and took off with rapid footsteps in Mark Lau's direction.

I sighed and smiled at my companion. "She's very enthusiastic."

"Very." He smiled back, looking pleased with himself.

Didn't he ever get sick of female admiration? *What a stupid question, Sarah!* Oh, well, no time to waste thinking about Mr Wonderful right now. My eyes scanned the room and though there must have been about two hundred people standing around, I immediately zoomed in on Jeffrey and Moira, who were talking to a group of older women. They were obviously networking and trying to sell their products.

Moira wore a floor-length red satin gown that clung to her petite figure and left very little to the imagination. Her long silky black hair hung smoothly down her back. Meanwhile, Jeffrey looked very handsome in his tux, and I noticed the women were ogling him. *Another charming bastard.* Those menopausal women didn't have a chance in hell with him, and I was sure before long they'd be eating out of his hands and begging him to take their credit cards for some of those wonderful anti-ageing products.

I was about to make a beeline for him when Mike's hand snaked out and restrained me by taking hold of my arm. "Let's have a drink first," he suggested, and nodded in the direction of a passing waiter, carrying a tray full of drinks.

"Champagne or orange juice," the waiter offered.

I made straight for the champagne, but Mike asked for something stronger. "Whisky and soda." The waiter nodded and walked off to fill his order while Mike's gaze turned to me. "Not a champagne sort of fellow," he explained.

"Maybe it's the bubbles," I remarked, thinking him too serious to go for what I termed a frolicky drink like champagne. Besides, the stuff was like soft drink. I gulped down the contents of my glass in one hit and looked around for another waiter.

"Steady on," Mike admonished gently. "You haven't even had anything to eat."

"Yes, Mum," I retorted with sarcasm. *How dared he think I couldn't handle alcohol?* Then, I remembered Monica's Christmas party, where I drank heaps of champagne to drown my sorrows after one of the many arguments I'd had with Jeffrey over Moira. Oh, no! My stomach churned uncomfortably as I wondered what Mike had seen me do on that night. Miserably, I wished I could remember.

Mike suddenly grabbed hold of my hand, bringing me back to the present. "Seeing as we're standing here, let's start making your Jeffrey jealous."

"He's not my Jeffrey!" I burst out. Then, more quietly, I added, "At least, not yet."

Just at that moment, I caught Jeffrey glancing our way, and Mike raised my hand to his lips and kissed the back of it. The move was perfectly timed, but I was too busy trying to quieten the thumping of my heart to enjoy the charade. After all, it was simply that—a charade. Mike played his part beautifully, which was more than I could say for myself.

When I managed to control the sensations his kiss left on my skin, I noticed Jeffrey merely smiled toward us and turned back to the group of women. I snatched my hand away from Mike's grip. "Well, that clearly worked." I was upset, mainly at myself for allowing his kiss to unsettle me. But my pretend date was not to know this.

He smiled in amusement. "Relax, will you? Give him time to get used to it. Besides, you said he always does business at parties, so what did you expect?"

I expected Jeffrey to come bolting across the floor to punch him in the mouth; but I could clearly see this wasn't going to happen, and the thought made me even more upset. Oh, I hated all men, and this damn menopause!

The waiter was back with Mike's drink, and I took the opportunity to grab another glass of champagne from his tray. I downed the drink quickly and snatched yet another before the waiter walked off to serve other guests. Mike frowned at me.

"You better keep your head," he warned, nodding toward Jeffrey and Moira. "The business discussion's over, and I'm going to say hello. Are you going to be okay here?"

"Sure," I replied, suddenly feeling relaxed. Champagne was great stuff.

Mike walked off in the direction of Moira and I watched as he struck up a conversation with her and Jeffrey. Another glass from a passing waiter and I was almost giggly. If nothing else, I thought, I was going to have some fun tonight.

Jeffrey noticed me standing alone—finally—and made his way over. He was scowling and my heart did a somersault. Perhaps, he was jealous. I gave him a dazzling smile.

"What's the deal with that fellow?" He frowned by way of greeting.

I felt elated. He really was jealous, so I decided to put on an act. "That's Mike for you. He's a bit of a flirt at times." I threw him a coquettish smile.

"I'll say." Jeffrey didn't sound too happy, and my love for him welled over. I couldn't go on torturing him like this. I had to set his mind at peace since he was so obviously upset over Mike's kiss.

"Don't worry, honey. It's nothing," I consoled him. "The kiss didn't mean anything."

He looked at me as if I'd grown an extra head. "What are you talking about? That guy had the nerve to interrupt us and then started chitchatting Moira!" He was clearly upset, and I did everything to keep my jaw from falling open.

"Moira! What's Moira got to do with it?"

"You just don't get it, do you?" He flashed me a look of anger, mixed with what I could only assume was distaste. "We're here to build a business, not climb the social ladder!"

I should've known he'd put the business above all else. He hadn't even noticed Mike kissing my hand earlier or if he had, he simply didn't care. "Excuse me," I uttered, trying to control my temper and feeling hurt at the same time. "Nature calls." I left him standing alone and weaved my way through the crowd while I managed to down three more champagnes on the way to the loo.

Mike found me a few minutes later, reclining on a chaise lounge near the buffet with my head resting on a cushion. "Why's everything spinning?" I giggled, and then laughed heartily when I saw his eyes looking into mine with a frown of concern.

"That's it. I'm taking you home. But first you're going to eat something."

Why is he so grouchy? I wondered in a haze of contentment as I watched him walk off and return within moments, holding a plate laden with mini spring rolls and steamed dumplings.

"I thought you left to take me home, Mr Grouchy," I remarked in a croaky voice before bursting into yet another fit of giggles.

Mike sat next to me and practically shoved the food into my

mouth. "You're not making any sense," he admonished. "I knew it was a bad idea to leave you alone."

I hiccupped in response, and his frown deepened. "If you're going to play games, you have to keep your head, Sarah. Look at you; you're drunk!"

"I'm ... not," I spoke in between bites, "not drunk ... just ... tipsy, and you're taking me ... home." Then, I giggled again and allowed him to go on hand feeding me. It felt marvellous.

Heaven only knows what the other guests were thinking, but I didn't care. Somewhere in the crowd, I espied Ping squinting toward me; and this time, she wasn't smiling.

CHAPTER 7

Mike inserted the key into the front door of my building and pushed it open.

"Thank you, I guess," I said, not sure what I was thanking him for. His behaviour toward me had been nothing but frosty since we'd left the ball. I didn't care. Right now, all I wanted to do was get out of my clothes, take a hot shower, and get to bed—hopefully to obliterate the disaster of the evening in deep slumber.

"Not so fast," Mike followed me into the small foyer. "I'm seeing you safely to your door." Then, he looked up at the old and narrow staircase in front of us. "Don't you have lifts in this building?"

"Are you kidding me? For the rent I pay, we're lucky to have a staircase at all, let alone a lift." I couldn't help but admire my wittiness and laughed at my own remark. At least, this showed Mr High-and-Mighty that I wasn't so drunk.

He frowned. God, he'd been frowning at me all evening. "Well, lead on, Macduff," he stated. "I'll be right behind you in case you fall."

I opened my mouth to tell him where he could go with his begrudging gallantry, but it was no use. He was already nudging me up the stairs.

There were two flights of stairs between each floor and by the time we reached my front door, we had climbed ten. Mike was not even breathing hard, but my lungs were ready to burst. How could this be when I was younger than him? Then, I reminded myself that charming bastards were not only devastatingly good looking; they were also super fit. I shrugged my shoulders in a gesture of helplessness. There was no point in thinking about this right now.

The guy was simply insufferable.

I turned to him, feeling rather despondent. "Well, thanks once again. Now can I have my keys?" I put out my hand to retrieve the keys from him, but instead of giving them to me, he proceeded to unlock the door and usher me in. Oh, no! He was invading my rat-infested inner sanctum, and there was nothing I could do about it. I shrugged my shoulders, this time in resignation. So be it. Nothing mattered anymore, not after the night's disaster. Besides, what was a rat or two? If anything, Mike would feel right at home with his little friends, and they could all celebrate the New Year together, I thought wickedly.

The door opened into the miniscule sitting-room-cum-kitchenette, which held two wicker chairs and a small glass-topped table in one corner and a stove, fridge and sink in the other. The only good feature in the room was the large plantation-style sliding door leading out to the rooftop terrace and the great view of the city skyline beyond.

Mike looked around but said nothing. I could tell he was not impressed with my grotty little kitchen, bare of cupboards save the doorless one under the sink. The linoleum floor dated back to the seventies and had certainly seen better days; and the rusty fridge and stovetop did nothing to add to its allure if there ever was any.

"Not much, but it's home," I commented, making a poor attempt at humour.

Mike gave me an encouraging smile. "Nice view," he remarked, moving toward the partly opened, sliding door. "May I?"

I nodded and he stepped out onto the large rooftop terrace, which was covered with all manner of pots holding various Chinese herbs and vegetables. "Yours?" he asked when I joined him.

"The landlady's mother's. It was part of the rental agreement— low rent in exchange for access to the terrace," I explained, daring him to comment on the arrangement.

He remained silent and instead looked up at the stars while I thought how unusual it was to have a clear night sky in heavily polluted Taipei. My building was located in the backstreets, just behind the central business district, and lights from office windows in tall skyscrapers winked back at us. "A very nice view," Mike finally spoke.

"Aaaahhhh!" I screamed as a furry creature scuttled across the floor and disappeared among some pots. "Sorry about that," I apologised. "The thing startled me. Fortunately, we have some great cats in the neighbourhood," I added, hoping he'd think the rat was an isolated incident.

"Well, you're bound to run into one of them now and again. After all, this *is* their year." His lightheartedness did nothing for my awkward feelings. I could tell he understood a lot more about the way I lived beyond the appearance of my small flat. Knowing Mike and his astuteness, I sensed he knew of my hand-to-mouth existence and the deep fear I felt that my business was not yielding the results I had expected. I wondered if it was possible for a person to smell another's fear and disappointment. Thankfully, he kept whatever comments he may have had to himself.

"How about some tea?" I turned back and headed for the sitting room, dispelling my thoughts and hoping there wouldn't be any more rats lurking about.

Mike followed me inside. "If you're not too tired."

I was tired. Tired and depressed. And I was about to break down and cry, but not in front of him. "Please, have a seat," I invited and busied myself with the kettle.

"So how long have you been living in Taipei?"

"About six months," I replied, my back to him.

"And exactly how did all this come about?"

I didn't answer straight away. Instead, I poured hot water into the teapot and brought it to the table along with cups, sugar and milk. "Help yourself," I offered, sitting down opposite him.

"Thank you." He gave me a warm smile.

I didn't know if it was the smile or the fact that I felt safe with him, but for some reason I knew I could confide in him. So as we sipped our tea, I found myself telling him things about my life I had told no one, except my best friend—and even Monica didn't know all the facts.

"I was going to be an arts teacher while I painted my way to stardom," I related wistfully, "but it didn't quite work out that way. So I taught for a few years in London and ran a gallery for a friend in my spare time."

Mike listened quietly, looking interested, and I went on, feeling rather relieved to be able to talk to someone who seemed to care about what I had to say. "Anyway, you know how it is. Time flies when you're having fun and before I knew it, I was in my thirties, fed up with dating commitment-phobic men and no longer happy teaching a bunch of school kids. It was then I became interested in health and decided to do a course in nutrition. I thought a change of career might be the thing."

"Well," Mike commented, "it's certainly a growing industry to get into, especially the anti-ageing side of it."

I glanced at him with surprise while he went on. "Multi-level or network marketing as some call it nowadays, seems to be the thing as far as distribution of quality products is concerned. In fact, many of these companies are growing quite fast and some already show a marked growth on the share market."

I was impressed he knew so much about the subject, but then he was an investment banker and bound to know all about the share market and which companies did well.

I continued with my story. "One night, a friend invited me to a dinner party. It was there I met Jeffrey and we got to talking. As you know, he only goes to parties for the networking." I smiled and Mike grinned in return. "So to cut a long story short, I signed up into his business. I guess I was lured by the possibility of travel, living in different countries, making a huge fortune and being financially secure for life." The latter came out sounding a bit forlorn.

Mike raised a querying eyebrow, but I went on before he could say anything. "Being new to it all, I worked closely with him, and that's how we became involved. Then, a year down the track, when the Taiwanese market was about to launch, he told our team this was the perfect opportunity for those of us who were serious about the business. He said we could make it big. So a whole bunch of us came here to develop the market." I drained my cup and refilled it. "Want some more?"

"Not for me, thanks." Mike regarded me quizzically, like I was some creature under a microscope. "What about Moira?"

I should've known this was coming. I sighed and thought there was no harm in telling him the rest. "Moira went to London with Jeffrey when he moved there from Singapore in his early twenties. Up until then, he'd been living with his parents, who are expats."

"So Jeffrey lived in Singapore until he went into network marketing?"

"Not quite. First, he went to university in London and

completed a degree in economics," I explained. "Always one to think outside the square, he decided network marketing was the way to go. A friend of his from London signed him up, and since then Jeffrey hasn't looked back. He's very good at what he does, you know." There was pride in my tone when I talked about him, despite what had recently transpired between us.

"I don't doubt it," returned Mike, "but you still haven't really explained about Moira."

Back to Moira, the woman who was a thorn in my side. "There's nothing much to say about her." I tried to keep calm. Thinking about Moira always agitated me. "She was Jeffrey's girlfriend in Singapore," I uttered, and abruptly changed the subject. "You won't believe this, but Jeffrey was quite shy before he went into network marketing."

"Hm." Mike looked doubtful but didn't ask me how I could possibly know this seeing as I'd met Jeffrey after his Singapore days. I suddenly realised I only knew what Jeffrey had revealed to me. I had no idea whether he'd been shy or not, and I wondered if Mike was trying to make me understand this fact. I tensed, disliking the turn the conversation was taking.

"So why is he being unfaithful to her now?" Mike again steered the conversation back to Moira.

I laughed, and he looked questioningly at me. "No, don't worry. I'm not drunk," I assured him. "The thing is Jeffrey was quite young and naive when they met, and Moira, being older than him by several years, trapped him into the relationship. She should've known better, of course," I sniffed disapprovingly. "In any case, when he tried to leave her, she threatened suicide—and she's been threatening ever since. She's always talking about jumping off balconies, slashing her wrists, stabbing herself with a butter knife or whatever," I stated, wondering if someone could really hurt themselves with a butter knife. I also wished I hadn't started talking about this, but judging by the look of fascination in his eyes, Mike was not going to let me off the hook just yet.

"And?" he prompted.

"And nothing." I felt fingers of tension starting to wrap themselves around my skull. "Jeffrey's too weak to leave her. She's been with him for years and though he's unfaithful to her, she just won't get the message."

"And this doesn't bother you?" Mike seemed surprised.

"Of course, it bothers me!" I tried to contain my frustration. Hopefully, the subject would soon come to a close. "But they no longer have anything together, except the business. Jeffrey says he's going to leave her when the time is right. He loves me, you know," I uttered firmly. "He says I'm the one."

"I see," Mike said slowly, pensively—with clear disbelief.

I felt my temper rise and hated the thought of having to justify my reasons for being with Jeffrey. "It's true. He's going to leave her. There's just too much at stake now because half the business is hers. But once Jeffrey builds up his team, he's going to purchase her half and send her back to Singapore."

"I believe you. Calm down," Mike stated in a placating tone. But he didn't look like he believed a word I had said.

"Don't tell me to calm down!" I cried, upset. "Jeffrey tells me to calm down; you tell me to calm down; meanwhile, I'm trying to get on with my life here, and I don't need to calm down!" The tension was now giving way to a pounding headache.

Mike was not put off by my obvious agitation. He simply went on gazing at me in that fascinated, disbelieving way, which made me feel more irritable by the minute.

"I think you should leave now," I said rudely. Tough luck if he was insulted by my manner. He didn't budge. "What is it?" I barked.

He regarded me with a serious look in his eyes. "Tell me one thing, truthfully; did you come all the way to Taiwan because of the business or simply to be near Jeffrey?"

Oh, God! He was asking me to bare my soul, and I wasn't ready for it. I blushed but didn't say anything. Instead, I became mesmerised by his delicious eyes and wished I could disappear into them, never to have to worry about anything again.

Mike broke the spell by answering for me. "So you just followed him around like a stray puppy. What kind of a cockeyed idea is that for growing a business?"

His criticism jolted me to the point of rage and gave me reason to lash out. "Who are you to judge, Mike Connor? Of course I'm growing the business. I'm working very hard and my team's growing. Soon, Jeffrey will leave Moira and all will be well!" I imagined I must have looked a mess with a face flushed in anger and eyes rapidly swelling with tears.

Mike got to his feet. "You're tired and in need of rest. Thank you for the tea."

I wasn't ready for him to go just yet. "Oh, so now you're leaving after you put me through the wringer with all your questions!" I wanted to hit him with something.

"Not really." He smiled kindly. "I just think you're far too smart a person not to see what's going on with Jeffrey and his empty promises. You simply need time to sort things out in your mind."

Could he possibly be more condescending? His steady green gaze got on my nerves. Mr Beautiful was full of himself. These charming bastards were all alike! And to think only moments before I felt safe in his company and ready to trust him with my feelings. I controlled my desire to throw something at him—an ashtray would be nice—and said with as much dignity as I could muster, "Well, thank you for seeing me home and good night."

"Good night, Sarah." Instead of walking toward the door, he suddenly pulled me into his arms and kissed me full on the mouth.

I was taken off guard and my struggles were puny against his strong arms. But let's face it—I wasn't necessarily struggling that hard. When his kiss deepened, I felt myself melt into him, and my traitorous arms wrapped themselves around his neck. My lips parted to give him free access to my mouth, but just as suddenly as he had pulled me toward him, he freed me with one swift movement, leaving me with an empty feeling and the burning imprint of his lips on mine. I looked into his tempestuous gaze, which held an almost savage passion, and all I wanted was to melt back into him.

"Perhaps, when you smarten up, you'll let me know," he said harshly and, before I could reply, he strode out, shutting the door behind him rather loudly.

Headache gone, but confused, I stood where he'd left me in my lonely and empty flat. Luckily, before I could examine my tumultuous feelings, my mobile rang, and I rushed to answer it. At this hour, it could only be one person.

"Hi." Jeffrey; calling from someone's bathroom.

I knew this was going to be bad news and my heart sank down to my gold sandals. "What is it now?" I was almost too afraid to ask.

"Hey, that's no way to greet me," he protested.

"Please, Jeffrey, don't comment on my manners when yours left a lot to be desired at the party."

"Okay, I'm sorry. I just got angry about your friend

monopolising Moira when she should've been working the floor with me!"

"Oh, of course," I returned sarcastically. "I forgot how we are all your slaves." For the first time, I almost felt sorry for Moira.

"What's got into you?" Jeffrey sounded annoyed all of a sudden. "You know we have to take every opportunity to grow the business. If you're not interested in growing your team, you may as well go home."

My heart jolted with fear. Was he going to break up with me? "Of course I'm interested in the business. It's just that—"

"It's just that instead of helping out Ping, you made a fool of yourself, drinking like a fish. Then, you left with Mike, the wonder flirt."

So he really was jealous! My heart leapt with joy. "I'm sorry about Ping," I lied. "I think Mike has a crush on me, and I had to get rid of him. I couldn't very well do this at the ball, could I? So I told him I wanted to leave because I had a headache."

"Whatever." Jeffrey didn't sound too concerned, and my heart sank again. He didn't seem to care after all. "Look, I just called to let you know I won't be able to see you for about a week. We're off to Tainan tomorrow morning. Moira has a big team there, and they need our help."

I gave way to anger. "So it's Moira again, the helpless nymph of the haunted forest!" I was past caring now. "Well, go! Go to Tainan or wherever it is you're always going to. I've had enough of this!" I threw the mobile across the room with such force it smashed through the kitchen window and went flying five storeys down to street level. Whatever happened to the days when you could simply hang up in someone's ear? I wondered despite my outburst. Then, I waited for the tears to come, as they usually did after one of my fights with Jeffrey, but surprisingly, they didn't start. Instead, and much to my annoyance, I found myself thinking about a pair of sea-green eyes and a body I wanted to melt into. *Grrr!*

Why was Mike Connor intruding into my thoughts? I hated the man. *What crap, Sarah! You just loved that sexy kiss he gave you. So who are you kidding? You wanted more.* Now, the tears came thick and fast, and I ran to the bathroom to wash my face with cold water. I hated charming bastards.

CHAPTER 8

The day following the Chinese New Year's party, I turned up on Monica's doorstep. "You can stay here for as long as you like," Monica offered.

After my fight with Jeffrey and my conflicting thoughts about Mike, I knew I had to run off somewhere neutral to think, and where better than Hong Kong? At least, Monica would lend a sympathetic ear. I didn't even bother to replace my smashed up mobile, either. Running away meant being out of contact with everyone, including Jeffrey and the disturbing Mike Connor.

Now, seated in the comfort of Monica's luxurious apartment, I recounted the story of Mike, Jeffrey, and the whole sorry tale of the New Year's party. Of course, I purposely left out the bit about Mike's body-melting kiss. This was a story I wasn't ready to share with anybody, not even my best friend.

"You need time out, Sarah," Monica advised when she saw the unhappy look on my face. "Let's examine the facts," she spoke in-between taking drags of her cigarette, "Jeffrey took off on you, and I don't think Mike's going to play the game anymore—not after you got drunk." She briefly glanced at me with faint disapproval. "Besides, it seems Moira and the business won this round."

I looked daggers at her. "Thank you for reminding me. And I wasn't drunk!"

Monica put out her smoke and refilled our wine glasses. "Tipsy then," she amended. "In any case, this is a game of strategy, and Moira outsmarted you."

"Hey!" I protested. "Whose side are you on?"

"Yours, of course." She smiled knowingly.

I knew that smile only too well. "Oh, no! Please don't tell me you have another plan. The last one backfired to kingdom come." I didn't think my heart could take much more of this.

"Well, if you want to give up, that's great," Monica remarked casually. "Jeffrey's a rat of the worst kind and you're better off without him." She drained her glass and poured herself another. Mine remained untouched.

"Okay, what's the plan?" I asked, against my better judgement. Much to my annoyance, I obviously wasn't ready to give up on Jeffrey despite what Mike had said and done. How did Mr Ego get into this? I asked myself as I eyed Monica's overflowing ashtray wistfully. Now that I was within easy reach of one, a big and heavy one at that, Mr Wonderful wasn't around.

"The plan is you play the same game Moira did."

"Huh?" I uttered, puzzled.

"Moira flirted with Mike," Monica explained as if to an innocent, "not in order to make Jeffrey jealous, but to show him that by becoming engrossed in another man she was at risk of being sidetracked from doing the business ... And what does Jeffrey care about most?"

The penny dropped. "Of course! How could I have missed it?" I exclaimed, refusing to admit that if Jeffrey cared mostly about the business, I was wasting my time with him in the first place. Who was I kidding? Of course Jeffrey only cared about the business—this was becoming more and more evident as time went on. So why was I hatching another plan in order to get him back? Talk about desperation! But my ageing hormones drove me on.

Monica threw me a sympathetic look, and I wasn't sure if it was because she read my thoughts or simply because she felt sorry for me. "You're too involved in this, honey. You can't see the forest for the trees," she stated in a bright and encouraging voice. "So now you need to take a step back and regroup."

I drank some wine, suddenly feeling the re-emergence of hope. "Moira's much more calculating than I thought," I acknowledged begrudgingly.

"She's just had plenty of practice, that's all," Monica remarked. "In my opinion, she's rather stupid for sticking around with a man who constantly cheats on her."

"The plan, please," I reminded her. I didn't want Monica to think the same thing about me. But perhaps I was the one being stupid for sticking around with a man who couldn't, or wouldn't, break up a relationship that seemed to be leading nowhere.

"Yes, the plan." Monica lit another cigarette.

I sighed with frustration. "Honestly, Monica, those things are going to kill you."

"Can't help it, honey. I think better this way. Mm." She took one long drag and expelled the smoke slowly, savouring every bit of it. "Well, the plan is you stay in Hong Kong for a while and start dating other men." She then added quickly when she saw me rolling my eyes in exasperation, "You have a team here, too, right?"

I nodded.

"And some members of this team talk to their counterparts in Taipei?" she continued.

"Yes," I replied, failing to see where this was going.

"Okay. So you start dating guys and then make sure some of these people know about it. Before long, word that you're out and about will get back to Taipei and to Jeffrey. He'll obviously become concerned, thinking you're distracting yourself with men instead of working the business; and if this doesn't shake him, I don't know what will." Monica was on a roll. "Before you know it, he'll dump Moira and fly over here to ensure you keep focused on your business."

What she said had merit. "And I'll have him all to myself again, like I used to in London. This'll give us a chance to start afresh." My heart filled with joy and I felt like shouting it from the rooftops. "Why, that's a brilliant plan! And I think it just might work."

Monica grinned. "What would you do without me?"

I went over to where she was sitting and hugged her. "What, indeed?" I was already feeling on top of the world. My dear friend had come to the rescue once again.

During the next few days, I went out a couple of times with male friends of Monica's. It seemed the men working for her were only too pleased to entertain an out-of-town guest on behalf of their boss. This was the excuse Monica had used to get me some dates without anyone feeling pressured. Meanwhile, I made sure a few of my team members knew I was busy dating and therefore didn't have much time for business meetings.

One of the team members happened to be a close friend of Ping's, so I could rest assured before too long, Ping would be spreading rumours in Taipei. After all, my behaviour at the Chinese New Year's ball would only lend confirmation in her mind that I had turned into a real floozy.

Ten days elapsed, and no word from Jeffrey. Then, I realised even if he wanted to call, he couldn't reach me. I hadn't replaced my old mobile yet; so I remedied this straight away and bought a new one, making sure I was in global roaming mode. Still no calls—not even from Mr Wonderful. But hadn't he told me to give him a call when I smartened up? What a nerve! As if I was going to call him. And even if I did call out of desperation, it wouldn't achieve anything. It wasn't like he was going to start dating me. He had only been my pretend date, a camouflage; an act to make Jeffrey jealous. I could not imagine he was interested in becoming my real boyfriend.

I shook my head in frustration. Why was I thinking of him in the first place? I didn't want him as a boyfriend. But the thought of Mike Connor brought colour to my face, and I felt my cheeks burn as I pictured myself in his arms, being kissed so very erotically, his tongue exploring my mouth …

I jumped at the sound of the incoming message alert on my new mobile and thankfully the image of Mike's kiss disappeared. I had twenty-seven messages waiting so I took a moment to clear my head from the intoxicating Mike and then dialled my voicemail service. The messages were from different team members, both in Taipei and Hong Kong. One of them was from Ping: "Hi, Sarah. We heard you're in Hong Kong. When are you coming back? Call me."

So, gossip travelled fast, I thought, pleased with myself. I smiled. Monica's plan was working, at least with my team anyway. There was still no call from Jeffrey. I tried to ignore my disappointment, without success, and wondered whether I was wasting my time going out with Monica's friends.

Deep down, I knew she was hoping I'd actually hit it off with one of them, and then it would be faît accompli—Jeffrey would be forgotten. Of course, this was too much to hope for. Firstly, I wasn't looking for another man; one was already enough to complicate my life. Secondly, the whole plan was to make Jeffrey come after me, not for me to find new love.

I checked my emails daily in the hope that word from him would come my way, but there was nothing except about fifty or so requests to meet up sent by men from an online dating agency to which Monica had submitted my details. Sometimes, I could kill her.

"I don't think this is working," I declared one night over dinner with Monica at a local Hainanese restaurant, which was a favourite of ours.

"Give it time. It's only been two weeks." She looked unconcerned, and I was faintly annoyed.

"Two weeks away from my business," I protested. "I can't afford to play games anymore. I don't even know if Jeffrey's heard that I'm over here."

"Didn't you say he was going to be away from Taipei?"

"Yes," I replied, "but only for a few days. He must be back by now." I felt impatient with her. However well meaning, she didn't know what it was like to live from week to week with only a small amount of money coming in.

She must have sensed my thoughts, however, because she said, "You're working with your team here, aren't you?" She was trying to be helpful now, but she still didn't understand how the business worked.

If I lost momentum with my team in Taipei, the whole thing could pretty much collapse overnight. My team members would lose their motivation to keep going by themselves if they had no one strong enough to drive them.

"The team in Hong Kong's fairly small compared to the teams I have in Taiwan and the UK. So I should be with one of those," I explained. Then, a new idea popped into my head. "I have it!" I exclaimed, almost making Monica choke on her Hainanese chicken rice.

"You have what?" She eyed me from the rim of her wine glass as she washed down a mouthful of food.

"I'll go back to the UK for a while. I've been in Taiwan for half a year now, and I want to visit my mother." I smiled knowingly at her look of incredulity. "I know what you're thinking, but I truly miss her. I've never been away from home this long."

"I can understand missing home, but Rosepurple?" Monica remarked with disbelief.

"Hey," I uttered, "she's my mother, you know! We may have totally different view points regarding my situation, but I still love her."

"Of course, I'm sorry. I didn't mean to be rude. It's just that since you gave up your place in London, you're going to have to bunk at hers—and I know how she sends you round the bend when she's driving home a point, especially such a sticky point." Monica's eyes widened to emphasise this.

She was right. Since I'd been dumb enough to let Rosepurple in on what I was doing with Mike, my mother had become highly suspicious of the whole affair and entirely disapproved of the situation with Jeffrey. Every time I spoke with her or emailed, she always asked why I had to hire a Lothario, as she put it, to steal away Jeffrey's girlfriend. She called Jeffrey a spineless wonder, and me, an insecure doormat. Rosepurple could really push my buttons, but only because in my heart of hearts, I knew she was right, which made me angry— whether at myself or at my mother, I couldn't yet say.

"Is she still over at Sloane Square?" Monica's question brought me out of my reverie.

"Yes. She loves that old flat." I sipped some of my wine and felt myself relax again.

"I always thought she was going to move to the country after your dad passed away."

"So did I. She used to talk about it often enough; but I guess once Dad was gone she felt the need to remain close to him. That was the place where they lived since they were married."

Monica smiled. "So we better not be fooled by her businesslike exterior. Rosepurple's a true romantic at heart."

We clinked our wineglasses in a toast to the indomitable Rosepurple, and I realised just how much I was looking forward to seeing her again.

"Don't look now," Monica exclaimed suddenly.

"What is it?" I asked with a feeling of expectation. Perhaps, Jeffrey had walked into the restaurant.

"Mike," Monica whispered quickly, pasting a wide smile on her face. "Look who's here," she greeted him while I sat as if set in stone.

Mike came up to our table and leaned down to peck Monica on the cheek while his eyes devoured me with a wicked glint in them. "Sarah," he said, "I never thought to find you here." He didn't kiss me; instead, he turned to the woman standing next to him, whom Monica and I had not noticed until now. "This is Gina, a colleague from our Hong Kong office."

Gina was a gorgeous brunette with cover girl looks; and for some unknown reason, my head started to ache all of a sudden. I put it down to the wine.

"Gina," Mike went on in his smooth, urbane, man-about-town voice, "these are two great friends of mine, Monica and Sarah."

Great friends, indeed. I had the sudden urge to throw my wine in his face, but I managed to control myself and gave the beautiful Gina the benefit of a polite smile.

"Nice to meet you," I spoke, my tone neutral.

"Likewise," returned Gina, trying not to look too impatient.

It was obvious she wanted to have Mike Connor all to herself. Well, she was welcome to him. Unfortunately, it seemed Mike had other plans.

"Monica," he said, all business now. "Gina's my deputy here at the bank. She's fresh out from the UK and wanted to discuss some logistics about setting up her household staff. I wasn't particularly happy with the agency staff I had when I lived here so I suggested she should speak with you."

"No problem. I have a wonderful housekeeper and chauffeur, Gina." Monica was all helpfulness. Then, she paused and addressed me with a wicked sparkle in her eye. "Sarah, would you mind giving us a few minutes? Perhaps, Mike can get you a drink."

I couldn't believe it. How did she manage to do it? In less than a minute, she engineered to remove me from the table and send me off with Mr Smug for a drink. Of course, I was helpless. It would be rude to refuse in front of everyone. Besides, Mike was already helping me out of my seat and guiding me toward the bar.

"Ping tells me you've been in Hong Kong these past couple of weeks," he remarked casually once we were out of earshot.

I felt myself bristle. "And since when do you question my team members?"

His smile was sardonic. "Who said anything about questioning your team members? Ping popped into my office, wanting to sell me some vitamin pack or other, and mentioned you'd gone off to Hong Kong— with no plans to return, I might add—and that you were dating other men."

I was flabbergasted. "Well, Ping's been a little busybody, hasn't she? She had no right to say that."

Mike ordered Pellegrino water for us and I pursed my lips at his assumption that I wanted a non-alcoholic drink.

"Which part?" He threw me a serious look.

"Which part what?" Annoyed by his condescending manner, I didn't understand what he was talking about. "And by the way, who says I want mineral water?"

"I prefer to talk to someone with a clear head tonight." He now regarded me with amusement.

"How dare you!" I felt my temper rise. "What makes you think I've had too much to drink?"

"Since I met you, sweet Sarah, you've always had too much to drink."

He smiled suavely, and I was rendered speechless at his nerve— and why did he call me "sweet"?

"So, which part?" he persisted.

I momentarily lost myself in his gaze despite my anger and my traitorous body swayed toward him. He steadied me by placing a hand on my arm.

"See what I mean? I think you've had too much wine already." He grinned wickedly.

That did the trick. I snapped out of my daze and took a step back. "I didn't have too much wine, Mikey Mike!" I saw his eyebrows rise at the name I gave him. "And I still don't know what you mean by 'which part'."

He threw me an indulgent smile, knowing I was simply parrying with words. The fact he knew it annoyed me even more. I hated it when I was so visibly readable to others, especially to Mr Wonderful.

Mike seemed happy to play along, however, and he repeated his question. "Which part did Ping have no right to talk about?" He handed me the water and I took it gratefully. Perhaps, I needed a clear head for this discussion after all.

"Well, if you must know," I sighed with exasperation at having to explain myself to Mr High-and-Mighty, "Ping doesn't have the right information and she's making assumptions."

"Okay, so *you* tell me," he went on.

"Tell you what?"

"Have you been in Hong Kong for two weeks?" he asked as if I were a child who needed things to be spelled out.

"Yes," I answered petulantly and looked into my glass as if all the mysteries of life were encrypted in the water bubbles.

"And are you returning to Taipei?" He raised a querying brow.

I hesitated at his questioning glance. "I'm … I have to go to the UK first. My team needs me there for a while," I improvised, "and I want to see my mother." At least, this was partly true.

"You still haven't answered my question. Are you returning to Taipei?"

God, the man could drive me mad sometimes! What business was it of his, anyway? He had the gorgeous Gina with whom to amuse himself. "Yes, I'll be back," I stated, but somehow I didn't feel so sure just yet.

"And what about these men you're dating?"

Boy, he didn't give up, did he? My temper flared. "That's none of your business. I didn't ask you about Gina, did I?" *That was silly, Sarah.* He would only think I was jealous, but I felt helpless. The man had this incredible talent for driving me to distraction.

"Gina's my deputy," Mike explained, unaware of what was going on inside my head. "She looks after Hong Kong for me while I'm in Taipei setting things up. I oversee the two offices and can't be in two places at the same time."

Halleluiah to that! I raised an eyebrow at him. "You don't have to explain your relationship with Gina to me." I felt I had the upper hand all of a sudden. I had actually reduced the great Mike Connor to having to justify his outing with a stunning-looking woman. My heart skipped a beat. It was just possible the overconfident and smug Mr Connor was jealous; and suddenly, I started to enjoy our little exchange, feeling somewhat triumphant.

Mike saw the look of glee in my eyes and his hand reached out to clasp my wrist. "I need a breath of fresh air. It's stuffy in here and it looks like Monica has plenty to say to my colleague. You won't be missed."

Before I could protest, he led me out of the restaurant to a small pier a few feet away, which overlooked the harbour and the bright lights of Hong Kong Island in the distance.

"What are you doing?" I tried to disengage myself from his grip, but his fingers were clamped tight and were there to stay.

"Listen to me." He swung me round to face him, and the proximity of his body sent a surge of heat through my whole being. "When are you going to stop this stupid game? Don't you get it yet?

Jeffrey doesn't care how many men you date, you little fool. If he did, he'd be standing here instead of me, doing this." He pulled me into his arms and his mouth descended on mine with a force that took away my breath while my limbs turned to jelly.

His kiss was deep, and suddenly his tongue was prying my lips open, plundering the depths of my mouth. My tongue met his in erotic play and the desire surging down to my core made me forget everything. Right at that moment, there was nothing in the universe except Mike and my incredible yearning to feel him inside me.

His hands explored my body with expert fingers, caressing my back, shoulders and neck. Then, a hand slipped inside the collar of my silk blouse and into the cup of my bra without any effort from him or resistance on my part. It seemed natural his hand should be there. My body arched toward his, wanting to fuse itself to him as his fingers teased my nipple and I moaned with such pleasure as I had never known before, not even with Jeffrey.

Jeffrey! My brain screamed the name to my body and I felt a cold chill travelling up my spine as I pushed away from Mike. In my dazed state, I realised the only reason I was able to free myself from him was that he let me go, even though he still kept a gentle hold on my arm. It was just as well because I didn't think I would have been able to stand on my own two legs.

I noticed Mike's eyes were clouded with passion and I could only imagine what was written in my own. He must think me a wanton tease, I thought, mortified; but he was the one who initiated the kiss. Yes, I reasoned in my muddled state of mind, but I hadn't exactly done anything to fight him off. I'd enjoyed it thoroughly, every bit as much as he had. *God, what is the matter with me?*

"I … We better go back inside," I managed to say in a normal tone of voice.

Mike remained silent when he nodded rather coldly and escorted me back into the restaurant.

CHAPTER 9

I felt Rosepurple's gaze on me while I sat on a chintz sofa chair in her lounge room, petting Mitzy, the cat. In front of me were a pot of tea and homemade scones with strawberry jam and clotted cream. I didn't know how Rosepurple did it—that is, change from a hardheaded, business super snoop into an old-fashioned, Queen-Anne-tea-set-using old lady, complete with pink fluffy slippers, all in the space of a few moments.

It was very cosy in the room with a fire lit to stave off the cold March weather, but all I wanted to do was to go to my old bedroom for a nap. My favourite childhood teddy bear, Ginnie, was still there, and I had a strong urge to get into bed and give him a big hug. Then, everything would be right with the world. But Rosepurple, it seemed, had other plans.

"Okay, Sarah," my mother stated firmly, glaring at me. "It's time you tell me what's going on."

Oh, dear. This sounds serious. I reached for another scone to buy myself some time before answering, all the while under her unswerving scrutiny. I took a bite of the delicious scone and washed it down with Earl Grey.

"Well?" Rosepurple prompted impatiently.

I regarded her with thoughtful eyes and wondered how a five-foot-nothing woman with red-rinsed hair, a bit on the plump side, could instill such fear in me. This ... hybrid person, for want of a better description, couldn't possibly be the sweet mother of my childhood. I squirmed in my seat with the knowledge that I wasn't going to be able to get out of this so easily.

"Really, Sarah," Rosepurple snapped, "what's gotten into you? Stop acting like a teenager in trouble and tell me why you're really here!"

"Fine," I sighed with resignation. "I just missed home and wanted to see you."

"Pish tosh!" she exclaimed with a harsh laugh, and suddenly I wondered whether she was going to turn into the wicked witch of the west and eat me. "The last time and only time, I might add, I heard from you was when you asked me to run a search on that nice man friend of yours, Mike Connor. So you didn't miss me at all."

Nice man? "I called you last week to tell you I was coming over," I reminded her, but the look she gave me made it clear she didn't believe a word I said. I ignored her accusing gaze and added, "And since when has Mike Connor become 'that nice man'? I thought you said he was a gigolo." I shook my head in indignation, hoping to distract her from asking more probing questions. Unfortunately, the look in Rosepurple's eyes didn't change as she regarded me with her no-nonsense manner, which confirmed, much to my distress, that she was bent on getting the truth out of me one way or another.

I gave in. "Okay, if you must know, things are not working out as I'd hoped with Jeffrey, and I wanted some time away to make him miss me." I winced when I realised how lame this sounded, but Rosepurple didn't lash back at me. To my surprise, she nodded as if all her suspicions had been confirmed.

"Figures," was all she said and then proceeded to pour herself another cup of tea. *Now what?* "Sarah, I have something to tell you that you're not going to like, dear."

Oh, no! This sounded bad, but for the life of me, I had no idea what she was talking about. Rosepurple put down her cup and gazed intently into my eyes from across the coffee table. "This Jeffrey is a real scumbag, dear," she announced so gravely that for a moment I thought she was telling me we were officially at war with another country—and where did she come up with these words: Lothario, gigolo, and now scumbag?

"What—?" I started to say.

"Let me finish, Sarah," my mother interjected. "Since your last call to me, I hacked into Jeffrey's email box and—"

"You did what!" I heard a voice exclaim with incredulity and realised it was my own.

"Are you deaf?" Rosepurple snapped. "I said—"

"I heard what you said, Mother," I interrupted while trying to come to terms with my disbelief at what she had done.

"Well, if you heard what I said, why are you gaping at me like a stunned mullet?"

I rolled my eyes. "Mother, why are you hacking into his emails? I never asked you to do that!"

"Never mind what you asked or didn't ask. I was worried about you, and it seems with good cause."

I saw her determined gaze and knew I was going to regret this, but I had to ask, "So what did you find?"

"The man's a scoundrel. He has no business ethics," she announced like I had full knowledge of Jeffrey's business affairs.

"What are you talking about?" I uttered, puzzled.

She gave me a look of impatience, but her tone remained matter-of-fact. "Well, I've been corresponding with him, you see, and—"

"What!" I jumped up from my chair at this piece of news and sent Mitzy scurrying for cover.

Rosepurple sighed with exasperation. "There you go again. Are you going to let me finish the story or keep saying '*what*' to every second word I say?"

I felt a sense of foreboding, but knew I had to remain calm and trust her. Rosepurple would never enter into correspondence with anyone unless she had a good cover. "I'm sorry. Please go on," I said, trying to control rising feelings of anxiety as I sat back down.

"I set up a fictitious business under the name of Maggie Day, and Jeffrey believes I'm one of his UK team members, about a hundred places removed from his immediate colleagues, of course." She smiled at her own ingenuity, confident I would be impressed. I was. She always worked meticulously, especially when snooping, and I sighed with relief. Rosepurple knew exactly what she was doing, I mused, even though she was using the next door neighbour's cat's name.

"Anyway," she went on, "I led Jeffrey to think my team leader wasn't helping very much, and because *Maggie* is new to this kind of business, she needs his expert advice on approaching new recruits."

God, she made it sound like network marketing was a cult instead of a business. "And?" I was really curious now.

"And he's been flirting with me nonstop, dear; like he's flirted with all the others, judging by his emails." She sniffed with disapproval. "Plus, he's asked for my pic."

Pic? Oh, God. "So what did you do?" I was almost too afraid to ask. How could Jeffrey do this when he didn't even take the time to send me one tiny email? What a bastard! I fumed inwardly but allowed Rosepurple to continue with her story.

"I sent him a pic of some soapie starlet he'll never recognise. She looked a bit like Posh Spice with blonde hair." Rosepurple seemed pleased with her cleverness. "Since then," she continued, "he's been emailing me daily. He gives me advice about the business while he flirts outrageously with me or I should say with Maggie."

I was itching for an ashtray. I needed something to throw. Instead, I remained dead calm in the face of my anger and listened quietly while my mother kept talking.

"He's now telling me all about his sorry state of affairs with Moira—the clinging, the fake suicides, and his noble attempts at encouraging her to grow and be independent." She leaned forward and gave me a conspiratorial look. "Did you know he's got plans to grow the business to double its size so he can break it off but still provide for her financially for the rest of her days? What a magnanimous gesture on his part." Rosepurple rolled her eyes in sarcasm. "She's like a sister to him, he says; and he loves her like one—only he thinks he's losing his heart to Maggie because *she's so understanding*, as he put it, and they have so much in common. He feels as if he's known her for a long time and therefore can express himself freely."

While my mother talked I felt an agonising pain pierce through my anger. It was my heart breaking. Luckily, she was so excited at imparting this information to me that she didn't notice the look of despair on my face.

"Now, he says he wants to meet Maggie on his next business trip to the UK," she stated and looked at me with compassion in her eyes. "Sarah, this man's no good for you. Why do you insist on wasting your time with him, dear?"

Snappishness and sarcasm, I could take from her any day, but when I saw the love and concern in her eyes, I knew I was going to break down and cry. "Excuse me, Mum," I uttered, getting to my feet. "I need to go to the loo." I escaped from the room before another word was said.

I lay in my bed, hugging Ginnie and feeling deep sorrow for the waste my life had been so far. A life marked by a broken engagement and a string of useless dates with impossible men—men who were not prepared to commit—although my ex-fiancé had married someone else, I reminded myself, feeling helpless.

Now, Jeffrey, the man on whom I had pinned all my hopes, looked as if he had been lying to me from the start. He'd told the imaginary Maggie he intended to buy off Moira's side of the business. This much was true, but why was he flirting with her when he was supposed to be in love with me?

All this time, I had believed the only thing standing in the way of our happiness was Moira, but now I was no longer sure. It seemed Jeffrey had one true commitment in his life—his business; and I was suddenly afraid this was the only thing to which he intended to commit. His relationship with me was merely a diversion because he was no longer interested in Moira; or at least, it looked that way, I thought glumly.

Moira had made too many demands on him by becoming clingy and constantly threatening suicide, and as a result Jeffrey lost his love for her. Now, I was the one making the demands, albeit of a different kind. I wanted commitment, marriage and hopefully to start a family before it was too late. These things were not so very different from what Moira had wanted; the only difference was the way in which she went about trying to get them.

It suddenly occurred to me Jeffrey might be frightened by all these things. Up until now, we had only talked about building the business and living together. But come to think of it, he'd never mentioned marriage at all. I had automatically assumed he would want the same things I did.

The torturous thoughts running through my head exhausted me, and my eyes started to close in the warmth of the room. Within moments, I sank into the wonderful oblivion of deep sleep.

***

I was at the Chinese New Year's ball and Mike found me reclining on the chaise lounge, resting my head. I was crying. Jeffrey and Moira were in the middle of the dance floor in each other's arms, kissing passionately while their team members formed a circle around them, each holding a vitamin pack.

All of this faded when Mike smiled at me and his wonderful eyes held a look of love in them so deep it astounded me. Then, as if magically transported through the air, we were standing on the small pier outside the Hainanese restaurant in Hong Kong, and he was kissing me with a passion I had never known. I felt the excitement of his touch pulsing through my body like an electric current and I leaned against him, only to feel the hot passion of his kiss coursing through my veins. I was drunk with desire. I was drunk with his touch.

We sank onto the pier floor, which was covered with soft, springy grass, dotted here and there with wild flowers. I stretched my arms above my head and Mike covered my body with his. He ravaged me with erotic kisses that moved from my lips down to my neck and naked breasts. I ran my hands over his back and smooth chest and felt his hard muscles under my fingers. Suddenly, we were completely naked, our bodies locked in passion.

"Sarah, Sarah," he whispered in my ear.

"Sarah, Sarah! … Are you asleep?" What seemed like a drumming sound seeped into my dream, and I was jolted awake by firm, loud knocking at my bedroom door and my mother's voice calling out to me. I was perspiring with the aftermath of my lovemaking with Mike. The dream had been so vivid my body still tingled all over with his touch.

"Sarah!" Rosepurple called out again.

"Yes," I replied in a sleepy voice. I wanted to go back to sleep and rewind to the last part of the delicious dream. What a great invention it would be if you could burn dreams onto DVD so you could watch them at a later time and relive the feelings all over again.

"Sarah, dear, do get up," my mother said through the door. "Your friend's here—that nice man, Mike Connor."

What! Mike Connor here? I was wide-awake and rushed to open the door. Rosepurple smiled, or grinning like a Cheshire cat, more like. "What's he doing here?" I whispered, agitated. "How did he find us?"

"Calm down, dear," my mother reassured me. "He got the address from Monica. Now, hurry up and come out, but first fix your hair. You look like you've been romping in the hay."

Rosepurple hurried off in the direction of the lounge room and thankfully missed the gaping look of surprise and embarrassment on my face.

CHAPTER 10

I entered the lounge room wearing a pair of faded blue jeans and a cream-coloured alpaca wool crew neck sweater. My hair was tied back in a short ponytail, and my face was bare of make-up. I thought I probably looked like a young girl roused from sleep instead of a woman on the brink of middle age. I hadn't had time to look in the mirror, however, and for all I knew I looked as horrid as the daughter of the wicked witch of the west. I hoped this wasn't the case.

Rosepurple was sitting adjacent to Mike and was in the process of pouring him a cup of tea while he petted Mitzy, who was resting contentedly on his lap. *Traitor!* I threw the cat an indignant look. She never went to strangers, but trust Mike to turn his charm on the idiot cat.

"There you are. At last!" remarked Rosepurple when she saw me. "Tea?"

"No thanks, Mum."

Mike looked very sexy in jeans and a black wool turtleneck top that hugged his well-defined muscles. I felt my knees grow weak. *Stop it!*

"Hello." He smiled charmingly. "You should have a cup. This tea's wonderful." Then, he turned to Rosepurple. "Thank you, Mrs Jamison. This is great."

She was all smiles. "Please, call me Edna."

I almost choked in disbelief. I couldn't remember the last time my mother had invited anyone to call her by her real name. She was either "Mrs Jamison" or "Rose" to all who knew her. My neck muscles started to grow tense. Perhaps, Mike Connor was the anti-

Christ and he sucked up everyone's soul through his charm. I shivered at the thought and berated myself for being fanciful.

"Well, it's time for Mitzy's dinner," Rosepurple announced to no one in particular and stood to take the cat from Mike. "I'll leave you two young people to talk. It was a pleasure to meet you at last, Mike."

Mike raised a brow at her remark. "The pleasure was all mine. I'm sure I'll be seeing you again, Edna."

Not if I can help it! I thought. One last smile from *Edna*, despite the daggers in my eyes, and she marched out of the room with Mitzy in her arms. I wanted to throw a cushion at her head.

"A pleasure to meet me *at last?*" The devil threw a wicked grin at me.

I flopped down on the chair my mother had just vacated and couldn't help blushing. Images of my recent dream intruded into my mind, and I hoped he wasn't able to see them. Of course not! I pushed the silly thought from my head. Mike wasn't really the devil; he just acted like one at times.

I ignored his question and fixed a serious gaze on him. "What are you doing here?" I almost barked, though I didn't mean to sound gruff. The man just got on my nerves.

"Nice to see you, too," he returned with a touch of sarcasm.

"Sorry. It's just that I was taking a nap. I'm still jetlagged from the trip."

"It's okay. I was only teasing." His smile made me glad I was sitting; otherwise, I was sure my knees would have buckled from under me. He had no right to come waltzing into my mother's home, looking devastatingly gorgeous, self-assured, and sexy as hell. Furthermore, he had no right intruding into my dreams.

The sexy, green eyes regarded me, waiting. "Sorry. I was miles away. Did you say something?" *Get a grip, Sarah!*

"Two apologies in a row," Mike stated. "It seems you'll now have to redeem yourself by coming out to dinner with me."

My heart skipped with excitement, but I managed to sound casual when I said, "So how come you're in London?"

He leaned back on the sofa and I couldn't help but notice his strong thighs, encased in denim. "Business meeting at head office; and seeing as I was coming all this way, I asked Monica for your number, but she didn't have it. All she could give me was your mother's address. Her phone number seems to be unlisted so I took a chance and came here in person. I hope you don't mind."

"Not at all." I did mind, but only because I felt inexplicably happy that he was here with me; and I wasn't supposed to feel happy. I was supposed to be grieving over my situation with Jeffrey.

"You still haven't told me about your mum being glad to *meet me at last*," Mike remarked.

I could see there was no way out of this. "Okay, so she knows about you." I tried to sound casual, like anything concerning him didn't matter. "She knew you were helping me out with the Jeffrey issue."

"You told your mother?" He looked surprised.

"What did you expect? You don't know Rosepurple," I blurted out and then looked at him in dismay.

He leaned forward, interest in his eyes. "Rosepurple?"

"Um … well, you see …" I wasn't about to explain to him that my mother was an international spook.

"I'm not seeing anything yet, Sarah. Why do you call her Rosepurple?"

Luckily, inspiration came to the rescue. "Mum has a website about cats and she uses the name Rosepurple in her forum." Lame, but believable. At least, I thought so.

"I see," he replied thoughtfully; and I had a sinking feeling he knew there was more here than met the eye. Thankfully, he let it slide. "Okay. Come on then."

"Come on, what?" I wished my heart would settle down.

"Dinner."

"Now?"

"It's only just gone eight," he declared. "Or do you have other plans?" It was like he was daring me to say I had a date with another man or worse still, with Jeffrey. Unfortunately, I had no other plans; however, I would have been over the moon if I'd had a date with Jeffrey tonight so I could wipe that enigmatic smile off the great Mike's face.

"I have to dress and …" I tried to search for an excuse to turn him down because I didn't trust myself going out anywhere with him, not after our last encounter.

"You're fine as you are. There's a great little Italian place in Notting Hill. You like Italian, don't you?"

I couldn't win—not when he looked at me with those eyes and

smiled with that mouth, which had given me so much pleasure, both in real life and in my dreams. Perhaps, I really was a wanton tease. I wondered how I could find this man so incredibly attractive and still be in love with Jeffrey. But right now, I didn't have the time to analyse my feelings nor did I want to do so. Mike was waiting for an answer. "Let me grab my coat," I said, making my decision.

The restaurant in Notting Hill was quiet, intimate and subtly lit, all factors conducive to a romantic dinner. The food was divine. We started with *tortino di carciofi*, a baked omelette with artichoke hearts, followed by *cuscinetti di vitello*, braised escalopes of veal with prosciutto and cheese stuffing. For dessert, Mike ordered *gelato di cocomero*, watermelon sorbet with pistachio nuts, chopped up candied fruits, and bits of chocolate—the perfect ending to a perfect meal. We drank a flowery red wine from the Tuscan region, although I limited myself to just one glass, and we finished off with espressos after dessert.

During the meal, we talked like old friends and discussed the differences between living in Hong Kong and Taiwan. Mike recounted some amusing stories about his domestic staff when he used to live in Hong Kong and even more amusing ones about his staff in Taipei with their more limited English.

"I can never get my housekeeper to buy the right food supplies. I say chicken, she comes back with duck. I say lamb and she brings me pork. Now, I just let her cook whatever she wants, even if she broils my steak instead of grilling it."

I laughed and could relate to what he said, which made me feel closer to him and very much at ease in his company. "I know what you mean. You should try ordering in Chinese and getting something totally different to what you asked for. At least, you have a housekeeper who has some knowledge of English. In most of the smaller eating places in Taipei, they don't speak a word of it. So when I'm not cooking for myself, I go to places where they have buffets, and even there some of the food looks like it's alive and might jump out of the soup to eat me instead of me eating it." I made a comical face when describing a creature with goggle eyes, peeking at me out of a bowl of soup, which had us in stitches. It struck me then just how easy it was to be in Mike's company.

He was unassuming, easy to converse with and had a wide knowledge of different subjects. Most importantly, not once did he mention money, business or networking, which were the only topics I seemed to discuss with Jeffrey whenever we were together. Even when I relaxed with him, the conversation was never about anything amusing or light. With Jeffrey, it was always business, business and more business.

I frowned at the thought, and Mike reached across the table to let his hand rest lightly over mine as he said softly, "What is it?"

I sighed and gazed into his eyes, now made dark by the subdued lighting in the restaurant, and wished I could dive inside them and lose myself in a world of sensation where romantic dinners with attractive men were the norm every day of the week.

"I'm okay," I replied, enjoying the feel of his hand on mine. "I guess I have a few decisions to make."

"Anything I can help with?" His concern seemed genuine.

"Not really. It's just …" To my horror, I felt a tear roll down my face.

Mike gave my hand a squeeze of reassurance and motioned for the waiter to bring the bill. "You're upset. Do you want to come back to my place for a nightcap? I see you hardly touched your wine," he commented, taking in my glass, which was three quarters full.

I hesitated before responding to his invitation, and he must have sensed this because he added, "I promise I'm a good listener."

I finally nodded. Somehow, I didn't want to go back to my mother's just yet. I couldn't face the barrage of questions I was sure Rosepurple would have for me about my date with Mike. So the later I went home, the better the chance she would be safely tucked away in bed and fast asleep.

Mike lived locally in a terrace house furnished in modern style and dotted here and there with antique pieces. He showed me into the lounge room and had a fire lit within moments while I sat back on a very comfortable cinnamon suede sofa. The style of the room was elegant, yet understated with muted colours, which complemented the furniture. It was the room of someone who appreciated the good things in life, but in a tasteful way. I espied a few oils of 18th century British painters and some valuable-looking books on a bookshelf lining one of the walls.

"What would you like to drink?" Mike asked once he got the fire going.

I looked into the crackling flames and started to relax. I was grateful he had left the lights off, except for a small table lamp in one corner of the room, which cast a golden glow. At least, if I burst into tears, he wouldn't notice my puffy eyes. "Cognac or brandy if you have it."

"Coming right up." He served the drinks from what looked like a Georgian drinks cabinet and then joined me on the sofa.

My heart jolted when I took the drink from him. His proximity was intoxicating and I took a large sip of the French cognac he had poured for me. I felt the drink burn its way down to my stomach and savoured the feeling for a few moments. "How come you're not married?" I blurted out and, for the life of me, couldn't understand why I wanted to know or what he must think of me for asking such a silly question.

He didn't seem to mind my curiosity and glanced at me enigmatically as if he was trying to figure out something about me. Then, he said, "I came close to it some years ago, but right at the last minute she decided to marry her career."

I was surprised. Mike Connor dumped over a career? Impossible. "What happened?" I was dying to know who would have dared to drop the great Mike for a job, and I couldn't stop myself from sounding overenthusiastic. Mike, however, did not seem to mind that I was being a nosey parker. He answered my question in all seriousness.

"She used to work with me. That's how we met, and shortly before the wedding she got an offer she couldn't refuse—head of a large investment bank in New York."

"And you wouldn't go with her?" I exclaimed with disbelief.

"I guess I could have, but by then I was already based in Hong Kong, and Gloria didn't want me to leave my career for her. Hong Kong was a big promotion for me, and she was the one who'd convinced me to take it in the first place. I was quite happy with my position in London, but she always wanted to experience life in Asia so she pushed for me to take the role."

I threw him a look of incredulity. "And then she dumped you?"

He laughed. "You'd like to think so, wouldn't you? But it wasn't quite like that. It just didn't work out in the end. I committed myself to taking on the job and was preparing for our life together in Hong Kong, when she backed out at the last minute. For her, it was a better offer, I guess."

"So you let her go," I stated in an accusatory tone. "Just like that."

His eyes regarded me with earnestness. "Sarah, when I make a commitment, I stick to it—and that's what I did."

"Even if it meant letting her go," I was quick to point out, wondering how he could let someone he claimed to love go so casually.

"Not quite. Remember she was the one who wanted Hong Kong in the first place, only to throw everything over for New York. She very quickly forgot the plans we made."

I noticed something like disappointment in his voice, and for some unknown reason this bothered me. "Like what?" I had to know what this man truly wanted out of life. Somehow, it really mattered to me.

"Like getting married, working hard for a couple of years and then coming back here to start a family—perhaps, even buying a house in the country to get away from it all. That's what we wanted or at least, what I thought she also wanted."

I must've been staring at him and for a moment his eyes held a gentle smile as he gazed back at me. "What is it?" he asked, looking somewhat amused.

"You wanted kids? Mikey Mike wants a family?" I couldn't help the tone of amazement in my voice.

He laughed heartily at the name I gave him. "Is that so strange?"

I thought about it, still under his amused gaze. "Well, not really … I guess."

"I have no living family," he disclosed, much to my surprise. "I lost both parents when I was quite young, and I was an only child. There were some distant cousins in Scotland, whom I never met, and that's it. So why wouldn't I want a family?"

"No reason." I looked at him with newfound respect. "I'm sorry. I didn't mean to make light of it."

"That's the third time you apologised to me tonight. I wonder what you can do to redeem yourself this time," he remarked in sly jest.

I smiled, beginning to like him; genuinely like him. "I'll get you another cognac," I offered and went to refill our drinks.

When I returned, we sipped our drinks quietly, looking into the fire, each wrapped in our own thoughts for a few moments.

The room was warm and I felt a wonderful sense of peace sitting next to him, sipping my cognac, and feeling closer to him than I ever had. Perhaps, it was the fact that I'd just discovered he was human after all. He had loved and lost. He was able to make a commitment and stick to it. He had laughed with me and was concerned when I became upset at the restaurant. I sighed, wondering why life was so complicated at times. Why couldn't Jeffrey be more like Mike?

"So are you going to tell me what upset you earlier?" his voice interrupted my thoughts.

I wasn't sure whether it was the warmth in the room or the cognac I'd been drinking, or maybe it was his concern for me. Whatever it was, I suddenly knew I wanted to be touched by him. I put down my glass and turned to face him. "I think I'm ready to redeem myself now," I announced in almost a whisper as I moved closer and touched his lips with mine.

Feeling daring, I pushed him back on the sofa and moved my body on top of his while his arms went around me, his mouth engulfing mine in a deep kiss that seemed to draw on the very essence of my soul.

We kissed long and passionately while our bodies molded together. Our hands wasted no time at all in exploring each other's body. Mike divested me of my sweater to reveal my white lacy bra. His mouth left a trail of kisses all the way down my neck until it reached the valley of my breasts. I moaned with hot desire and pulled at his top so he would take it off. I kissed his chest and nipples and felt them go hard at the touch of my tongue. This aroused me so much I sat astride him and unclasped my bra to let him see the ripeness of my full breasts. He reached out and massaged them tenderly, and then his mouth tasted my nipples, sending electric shocks of pleasure through my body.

His touch seemed to burn on my skin and I was carried to a place where only erotic sensation existed. With trembling fingers, I unzipped his jeans and made to pull them down, but I couldn't do this on my own and looked to him for help.

"God, I want you so much," he whispered in my ear.

"I want you, too." I heard myself respond as if from a faraway place.

All I wanted was to be naked under him and have him inside me. I felt his fingers undo the studs on my jeans, and I helped by pulling them off. Then, I lay alongside of him, naked but for my underwear. His hand made its way down to my panties and soon his fingers found the soft, downy area between my legs. I moaned and arched into him, feeling the hardness in his pants pressing into me.

"Take me now," I uttered hoarsely.

Then, abruptly, everything stopped. I felt myself being gently pushed to a sitting position, and Mike was handing me the clothes that had earlier been thrown on the carpet with such abandon. "Dress yourself," he instructed, his tone rough.

I shook my head as if to clear my jumbled thoughts. *What happened?*

Mike put his top back on and zipped up his jeans. "We need to talk," he stated to the speechless and stunned person who felt like she was someone else, but in actual fact was me. Mike switched on the main light in the room and I shielded my eyes from the glare as I wildly wondered what had gone wrong and whether I had offended him in some way.

Unfortunately, I couldn't find my voice and once again, to my horror, I felt tears streaming down my face. Mike pressed a glass of mineral water into one of my hands and a bunch of tissues in the other. He sat next to me and turned me to face him by taking hold of my shoulders. I felt like a rag doll.

"Sarah, you have to listen to me," he implored.

I merely nodded, too dumbfounded to speak.

He said, "There's nothing more that I would love to do right now than to make love to you—but not like this."

I finally found my voice, although it came out sounding very faint. "Like what?"

"With your head full of Jeffrey," he answered and smiled gently at my wide-eyed look. He added, "Don't think I don't know you're on the rebound. I'm not sure exactly what happened between you, but I do know you're still thinking of him, and I won't have you throw yourself at me. I'm not a compensation prize."

His reasoning stung—perhaps because it rang true. I was too shocked to reply. Mike gave me a serious look and said, "You're a beautiful and desirable woman, but I don't want another man's leavings."

Thankfully, anger started to well up inside me and my tears disappeared while my face grew hot with indignation. This time, my voice came out sounding loud and clear. "How dare you accuse me of throwing myself at you?"

"Sarah, I know about the emails and Jeffrey's flirtation with Maggie Day," Mike dropped the bombshell.

Rosepurple! My brain screamed. How could she tell him? And how dared Mike Connor charm an old lady to pump her for information? An overwhelming feeling of rage swept through me and I shook with it. "You're … you're …" I couldn't find the words. "You're … despicable!" I finally yelled. "And you flatter yourself. I'm not some piece of garbage thrown away by another man, you know. I'm … I'm me, and … and …" And then, I burst into tears and ran out of the room and out of his house.

Although I was dressed in jeans and a sweater, I hadn't had time to put on my shoes or jacket, so the cold air outside hit me like a wall of ice. Luckily, I espied a taxi and flagged it down before Mike was able to make it to the front door.

As the taxi drove off, I saw him standing in the middle of the road, my jacket and shoes in his hand.

CHAPTER 11

"**I**'m so sorry, dear," said Rosepurple when I confronted her the following day. "I thought Mike knew all about the situation with Jeffrey, so I didn't see any harm in letting him know about the Maggie Day thing. You did say he was helping you out after all," she reminded me.

I sat in Mum's country-style kitchen, sipping on a cup of tea and looking out at her small back garden through the French doors of the ground floor flat. Spring was in the air, but the wind was still very cold and I shivered while trying to work out why I felt so great a loss after the episode with Mike.

I had come in very late the previous night and, thankfully, my mother had already gone to bed. I was relieved I hadn't had to explain my missing shoes and jacket.

"That's okay, Mum," I sighed, realising it wasn't her fault. Mike seemed to have this effect on all women, even the older ones, and soon the ladies would find themselves telling him everything he wanted to know and more. My mother hadn't been aware of how much Mike knew about my situation and she'd probably thought confiding in him was harmless.

"I guess if I'd known he was going to visit, I would've warned you not to say anything. It doesn't matter anyway," I said with a touch of sadness in my voice. "He's not playing the game anymore and I'm not likely to see him again." I sighed again, listlessly.

My mother frowned. "Honestly, Sarah. I know this is none of my business, dear, but why do you insist on chasing after Jeffrey? He's bad news."

Why indeed? I felt tired and disheartened with the whole situation.

Chasing after Jeffrey, as my mother put it, was proving to be a huge waste of my time. Besides, I had to get back to my business if I wanted it to grow. As for Mike, I blushed as an image of what had happened the previous evening flashed into my mind; I cringed at the fact that I'd thrown myself at him, only to be rejected. I felt mortified every time I thought about it, and I'd been thinking about nothing else since I opened my eyes this morning.

"I'm not chasing after Jeffrey anymore, Mum," I announced to my concerned mother, feeling empty. "So please don't worry. I only need time to think about things."

Rosepurple regarded me with what looked like pity in her eyes, but she didn't comment further. Just then, the doorbell rang and my heart stopped. "You get it." I stood abruptly and walked to the kitchen door. "I have to go to the loo."

I escaped as fast as my legs could carry me without arousing suspicion. The last thing I wanted to do was face Mike Connor right now, and something told me he was the person knocking at the door. I was wrong; and this was confirmed a few minutes later when Rosepurple knocked on my bedroom door and called out, "A package arrived for you, dear."

I had been about to check my emails and sighed with both relief and disappointment that it wasn't Mike out there. So he hadn't come after all. I felt peeved and went to open the door.

My mother handed me a large box. "Probably more of your vitamin packs," she remarked and walked off.

I sat on the bed and opened the box with trembling fingers. I knew who had sent the package. When I lifted the lid, I saw my shoes and jacket lying neatly inside together with an envelope. I opened it and read Mike's note:

Sarah,
In your hasty departure you left these behind. I thought you may want them back.
Yours, Mike

I couldn't believe it. No mention of what had happened between us. No apology for the way he'd practically pushed me off him and told me he didn't want another man's leavings. Nothing! And to think I'd been feeling miserable at the thought of not seeing him again.

I ripped up the note, imagining I was ripping up Mike Connor instead, and reproached myself for having thought of him as human. The man had a heart of stone, and he was welcome to it. As far as I was concerned, I wanted none of it. I'd had enough of smug bastards—first Jeffrey and now Mike.

I disposed of the box and returned to checking my emails and I suddenly espied one from Jeffrey. My heart did a little somersault. Oh, God! With all these skips and missed beats, I was having a very difficult time of late. While I read the email, I started to feel a little better and my loving feelings for Jeffrey made a comeback.

"Darling Sarah," he wrote, "I can't imagine what you must think of me, but please don't delete this email. Read it through and if you don't reply, I'll understand.

"First of all, I want to apologise for not contacting you earlier. It's been hell in Tainan. Moira made another suicide attempt when I tried to explain I wanted to buy her half of the business and break off our relationship."

I rolled my eyes as I read this and wondered why Jeffrey bought into it when Moira never succeeded in killing herself. Even a child would realise she was only doing it to attract attention.

I read on. "Well, you can just imagine what followed—tears, hysterics, the lot. I had to call the doctor to have her sedated, and in the meantime I attended a number of presentations for the team. It was pretty much 24/7 and I hardly had time to sleep, let alone write."

Yes, but he'd had time to write to Maggie Day, I thought in anger. I read the rest of the email with mixed feelings. "Finally, when I got back to Taipei, Ping told me you'd gone to Hong Kong. When I rang your mobile, I couldn't get through so I telephoned Monica, who told me you'd gone to the UK. I couldn't reach you there as your mobile was shut off. I didn't have your mother's number so as a last resort, I wrote this email."

At least, he was telling the truth here. I had switched off my mobile on arrival to the UK because I didn't want any calls from anybody connected with Jeffrey or the business. Jeffrey must've just missed me when he'd tried me in Hong Kong. My heart warmed to him once again.

"Anyway, my dear Sarah, I just wanted to say I miss and love you. Please come back to Taipei and try again. I took it upon myself to pay three months rent in advance to your landlady and purchased a plane ticket for you. Try not to be mad at me; it's the least I could do after the way I treated you. Darling Sarah, I hope you'll come back. I wait on tenterhooks to hear from you. All my love, Jeffrey."

I was blown away. This was a complete turnaround from the Jeffrey I thought I knew. Joy filled my heart. I had been right in the first place—he did love me! He truly loved me and wanted me with him. It wasn't his fault Moira was constantly trying to commit suicide at the drop of a hat. Jeffrey was trying to do the right thing by her, and I loved him all the more for it. If he'd been more like Mike, he would've thrown Moira out on her ear without any thought as to her feelings. And to think that only last night I wished Jeffrey would be more like him. God forbid! At least, Jeffrey was trying to do the honourable thing by the woman he'd been with for so many years. I acknowledged that, and although this wasn't so convenient for us, at least he wasn't discarding her like a piece of garbage.

I sighed in wonder. Jeffrey truly loved me. He'd just told me. He'd even paid my rent in advance and bought me a plane ticket. What man would do this if he wasn't serious about having a relationship?

With my decision made and a happy smile on my face, I started clicking away at my keyboard in reply to his email.

***

"But Sarah, dear, is this wise?" Rosepurple asked that evening over dinner at a small Chelsea café she frequented regularly.

I sighed, wishing I didn't have to justify over and over again why I'd made the decision to return to Taiwan. "Mum, he's paid for everything. Why would he do this if he had no intention of trying again? Besides, I told you I'm not chasing after him anymore. This time, he's chasing after me."

"The man has plenty of money; otherwise, he wouldn't be able to buy half the business from his partner," my mother argued, obviously not impressed with the fact Jeffrey was allegedly chasing after her daughter. "So what's three months' rent plus a plane ticket to him?"

I started to feel irritated but didn't want to have words with her right now. My mind was made up. I was flying back to Taipei to try again; and together, Jeffrey and I would hopefully find a solution to the Moira problem.

Later in the evening as I packed in my room I thought once again over the incident with Mike Connor. I couldn't get past the way I'd thrown myself at him and asked him to make love to me. Perhaps, Mike had been right in rejecting me because I was on the rebound. The fact was that I truly had been feeling upset over Jeffrey. Then, being thrown together with Mike, and his being so caring and sympathetic to my feelings, not to mention charming, simply made me lose my head.

I hated to admit it, but in retrospect Mike had been right; and I was now relieved he didn't make love to me after all. If he had, I couldn't imagine how I would be feeling at this moment, especially after Jeffrey declared his feelings for me and asked me to come back. Besides, I found it disconcerting to think what Mike would have made of me, jumping out of his bed and into another man's. He would've thought me flighty, a wanton tease, someone incapable of making a commitment, just like his ex-fiancée—only she'd thrown him over for a job and not another man.

At the same time, I reproached myself for musing over the great Mike Connor after the way he treated me—calling me another man's leavings, and then sending my shoes and jacket via courier the following day. He hadn't even had the decency to call around himself and return my belongings. I asked myself whether I'd really wanted him to do this in any case. Unfortunately, and much to my chagrin, the answer was a resounding yes.

As I threw my clothes into the suitcase without bothering to fold them, it became obvious to me that I wanted to see him again even though he'd made it more than plain how he felt about me. Yes, he wanted me; but not as some other man's leavings.

I had no doubt in my mind he wanted me. He made this more than apparent by the way he'd reacted to my touch, just as I'd reacted to his. My cheeks burned at the thought of how close we'd come to going all the way, and I was grateful he stopped in time. *But am I really?* Before I could answer this question, I shut the suitcase with more force than was necessary and sat on my bed, wondering why I was no longer feeling ecstatic about returning to Taiwan and, more importantly, why I was mooning over the hateful Mr Connor.

Chapter 12

"I'm not getting a good feeling about this, Sarah." Monica lit a cigarette, much to my annoyance, as I tried to make out the outline of her face from across the coffee table in her smoky lounge room.

I had accepted her invitation to stay on for few days in Hong Kong instead of going straight through to Taipei. This made sense because I wanted to catch up with my Hong Kong team before I went back. Once in Taipei, I would have no way of knowing for sure how long it would be until I returned.

Despite Jeffrey's generous gesture of paying for my rent and plane ticket, I was running very low on cash; and the time I'd spent away from my Taiwanese team had already resulted in a number of people dropping out of the business. In fact, according to my last team report, and much to my surprise, a large number of people had dropped out since I'd left Taipei the previous month.

"I have to get back to my team," I told Monica. "I've only been gone less than a month and already I lost close to forty percent of my people. Even Ping's on the verge of leaving, and she's one of my strongest team members. It was lucky she called me before she made her decision."

Monica listened to me with an expression of exasperation on her face. "So what are you going to do; stay there forever? If you can't even leave them alone for a month, how do you propose to keep the team going in the future? You'll have to become a slave to the business."

I sighed with impatience. "This isn't a regular job, Monica. It's all about motivating people to do well and building a strong team with confident leaders. Once the structure is in place, I can move on. Look at my UK team; they seem to be doing okay without me." But this was a lie, and I frowned momentarily. Even while I was in London I noticed some of my team members dropping out of the business, though nowhere near as many as the amount of people from my Taiwanese team. Therefore, I convinced myself the reason my UK team had fewer dropouts was because it was more established and the members didn't need me as much for support. However, a vague worry about the downturn in the business as a whole remained at the back of my mind.

"I still don't like it," Monica stated, puffing away at her cigarette.

"Jeffrey wouldn't have paid for me to come back if he didn't love me," I argued. "I owe him another chance. Besides, I still love him." I was fed up with having to explain my motives for going back to Taipei—first to Rosepurple and now Monica, to say nothing of the insulting Mr Connor, who had not even made an effort to call me in order to find out how I was getting on. Suddenly, I felt irritated.

"What's going on with Mike?" Monica asked; and I wasn't the least bit surprised she sensed my feelings. After all, they probably stood out like a beacon.

"What about him?" I made to sound casual, perhaps too casual to fool Monica.

"Come on, Sarah!" Monica remarked, annoyed. "Mike Connor doesn't fly halfway across the world unless he's after something. He's super busy right now, what with overseeing the Hong Kong branch and setting up in Taipei."

"For your information, Mike was attending a meeting at his head office. This was his reason for going to London," I stated for the record. "Besides, I thought this woman, his deputy … what's her name? Anyway, I thought she's running the Hong Kong side of things for him."

Monica smiled mysteriously, and I felt even more irritated. I knew she saw right through me. "Her name's Gina, as you well remember, and I believe you're jealous of her. So spit it out. What gives with Mike?"

Sprung! I did not want to explain about Mike, but I owed it to her. Monica had been supportive throughout the whole ordeal and she deserved some kind of explanation. I sighed with resignation and noticed she was all eyes and ears. She hadn't even lit up another cigarette.

I gulped. "There's ... I mean. I ..." I really didn't know where to start.

"Well? Out with it." She looked expectant, and still intent on trying to fix me up with the vexing Mike Connor at all costs.

"I threw myself at him and he rejected me," I blurted out all of a sudden and felt my face grow hot.

Monica looked stunned, but only for a moment. She recovered very quickly, I noted. "Oh, my God!" she screamed in delight. "And I thought it was going to be the other way around—Mike making a pass at you. This is priceless!" Her face wore a wide grin.

"Before you run away with your imagination, let me clear things up," I interjected. "There's been a strong attraction between us, you see. It's been there from the start ... I think, anyway." I still felt confused about my feelings for Mike, and right now there was grief in my heart for the way we had parted. This clouded my feelings even further. "Well ... he kissed me on the night of the New Year's party—"

"You never told me this before." Monica eyed me accusingly.

"I wasn't ready to tell anyone. I didn't think anything of it at the time." This wasn't true, either, but it would have to do. "Then, remember the night we saw him at the restaurant with Gina? Well, he kissed me on that night, too."

Monica loved what she heard, judging from the expression of delight on her face, and I didn't want to go on. I felt humiliated enough as it was. I cleared my throat. "To cut a long story short, we had dinner in London and one thing led to another, and—"

"You slept with him!" she shrieked with excitement.

"No!" I denied vehemently, colouring once again. Just the thought of Mike touching me was enough to make my body cry out with desire; and I decided I hated my traitorous body. "I almost did, though." I explained further as I saw Monica's expectant look. I knew she wanted to hear every detail. "I was feeling really low about the situation with Jeffrey and we ended up at Mike's place. But in the end, he rejected me. He told me he didn't take women on the rebound and certainly not another man's leavings." This last bit still had the power to hurt and to my dismay, I felt tears rise to my eyes. Luckily, I suppressed them just in time.

Monica regarded me with sympathy. "At least, he was honest

with you, Sarah. Imagine how much worse you would've felt if he'd taken advantage of the situation."

"You're right," I admitted. "At first, I was angry, but when I had time to think about it, I realised it was just as well he put a stop to it."

"So Mike Connor falls at last," Monica remarked with a smile of satisfaction on her face.

"What's that supposed to mean?" I knew I sounded defensive and perhaps a little bit hopeful.

"Honey, you are so naïve!" she exclaimed. Then, in a confiding tone, she continued, "I've known Mike for a long time, and I can tell you he's never done this much for anyone. If you'd been any other woman, he would've slept with you and that would have been that. You'd both have gone your separate ways. He's been like this since his break up with Gloria. He thinks women are toys to play with and then discard. This is why I thought he was perfect for your little project. I knew he wouldn't have any qualms about charming Moira and then dropping her like a sack of potatoes."

"What a charmer," I uttered, rolling my eyes. "But don't forget you were trying to set me up with him. So, thank you, Monica, for sending me a smug womaniser." Then, I added thoughtfully, "No matter what your motives were, however, I don't think he cares for me. Why should he? He knows I'm in love with Jeffrey."

"God, Sarah, you sound as if you were born yesterday. Of course, he cares for you. Why else would he have stopped when he did? It's obvious he wants you. He's kissed you more than once in the past, so he certainly doesn't find you repulsive."

"Well, that's nice to know at least, but it doesn't matter now." There was a note of sadness in my voice I didn't care to analyse so I turned to resentment instead. "He doesn't want another man's leavings, remember?"

"And this seems to bother you a lot," Monica observed, smiling knowingly. "Could it be you're developing feelings for him?"

"Never!" I denied quickly.

"Hm." Monica regarded me with doubt and then remarked pensively, "So what's to be done now?"

I glared at her with incredulity in my eyes. "What the hell are you talking about? There's nothing to be done. I'm off to Taipei to be with Jeffrey, and as far as I'm concerned I never want to see the precious Mr Connor again."

In my heart of hearts, I knew this was a lie. I did want to see him; and this made me so angry I seriously considered taking up smoking if I knew for a fact that it would help with my frustration.

CHAPTER 13

Jeffrey was waiting when I walked through the arrivals gate at the airport, and my heart leapt with joy as he took me in his arms and kissed me thoroughly. I smiled in anticipation and looked into his baby blues. Finally, I was where I belonged, and life looked brighter by the minute.

"I'm so glad you're here," Jeffrey said in between kisses. "I honestly thought I'd lost you."

We went back to my flat and spent the afternoon making up for lost time, deliciously so. I realised just how much I had missed his dear face, framed by his shiny black hair and the deep blue of his eyes.

"I really missed you," I told him later over coffee as we sat out on the terrace, enjoying the warm April sun. "You know, it was very difficult coming back," I confessed. "I wasn't sure whether I wanted to go through this whole Moira thing again, but I couldn't let go without making one last effort."

He reached out and caressed my face. "I'm glad you did, and I have good news!" His eyes brightened up with excitement. "I'm now in a position to buy her out."

I nodded expectantly and waited for him to go on.

"It seems she's thinking about it seriously," he explained. "So we had a long talk once she recovered from her ordeal."

I couldn't help rolling my eyes at this comment. Thankfully, he didn't notice while he talked on. "I tried to make her understand that there's nothing between us anymore and that I want to get on with the rest of my life. It looks like she accepts the situation now, and she's asked me to give her some time to work out what she wants to do regarding the business. Then, I'll start negotiations with her."

It occurred to me I should be jumping up and down with joy at this piece of news. Instead, I felt unusually calm, and I put it down to the fact that seeing was believing. I had become quite cynical of late, but I put on a smile for him lest he read my thoughts. In a cheerful voice, I remarked, "I'm glad to hear it."

"In the meantime," Jeffrey went on, "we have to keep working hard to make sure our teams stay strong."

"Yes. I noticed there was quite a drop in my team since I left," I commented and was surprised when he did not berate me for it.

In the past, he would have made a big deal about something this serious and subjected me to a long lecture about the whys and wherefores of growing the business. I dared to give hope to the thought it was now possible that he'd changed a little, realising there was more to life than business. Despite this, I still didn't feel excited about the prospect that he had begun to change after all this time—and I couldn't quite work out the reason why I felt this way.

I was a hair's breath away from having what I wanted, what I had been fighting for all this time; and yet, I didn't feel anything much at all. Plus there was something else—the business with the imaginary Maggie Day. This hadn't yet been cleared up, and I wondered whether my mother had exaggerated the situation in order to distance me from Jeffrey. Watching him now, looking so relaxed on the terrace, I couldn't believe he would go to all the trouble of getting me to come back, and take steps to break it off with Moira, only to carry on a flirtation with Maggie. Still, I had to know for sure. So I resolved to broach the subject without arousing his suspicion. As far as he was concerned, I was not meant to know anything about the Maggie Day situation. Therefore, I would have to be careful with what I said.

"What is it?" Jeffrey asked, noticing the frown on my face.

"Nothing important," I replied and decided to go for broke to test him out. "It's just that I ran into someone who knows you in London. I believe she's a team member of yours. She happened to be at a meeting I attended." I watched his face for a reaction, but his expression remained impassive.

"And?"

"I think she said her name was Margot … no … Margie. No,

that's not it." I made like I couldn't remember the name to give him the chance to jump in with the right one; instead, he waited for me to go on. "Maggie! That's right. Maggie Day," I declared.

"So what about her?" his tone sounded casual, his expression still impassive. I decided then that there was a high probability Rosepurple had exaggerated the whole thing in her concern for me.

"Oh, nothing earth shattering," I replied in an offhand way, "only that she was raving about you and said her immediate team leader wasn't very helpful, and that you were taking the trouble to coach her online. I just thought it strange you'd do this seeing as the team leaders are supposed to take responsibility for their own people."

Jeffrey shrugged his shoulders. "Well, sometimes team leaders get a little too complacent about their members and think newbies can cope with anything. This is how team members end up dropping out. They don't see the support from their leaders," he explained, his voice becoming impassioned all of a sudden. "So I decided to take Maggie under my wing and coach her online. At least, it'll motivate her to grow the business."

What he said made perfect sense, but something still niggled at me, and I found myself going a step further. "Surely, this must be a difficult thing to do, unless you make the time to go over there in person and work with her. Remember how you used to work one on one with me when I was new?" Once again, I waited for his reaction but was disappointed, and somewhat relieved, when he took it in his stride, causing me to decide he must be telling the truth after all.

"Yes, I know," he responded. "The thing is, Sarah, once you get to my level and have thousands of team members under you, you can't take the time to work with each one individually. I'm doing the best I can for Maggie long distance. In the end, though, she'll have to work with her own team leader, whom I intend to speak to and find out why he isn't supporting her."

Jeffrey wasn't giving anything away, but this did not matter as a bolt of panic shot through me. How was he going to speak to anybody when Maggie Day was purely an invention? I knew Rosepurple had placed her under a real person in Jeffrey's team. But when Jeffrey actually contacted the team leader, it would all come out in the open. The team leader would deny knowing anyone named Maggie Day. *Oh, my God!* I had to get on the phone to my mother as soon as possible and tell her to make out like Maggie was dropping out of the business. Rosepurple would have to send an email to Jeffrey from Maggie, saying she'd decided the business wasn't for her.

Jeffrey's mobile rang just then and he answered in Mandarin. It was Moira. My heart plummeted. I hoped things weren't going to start all over again, but the call was short and there seemed to be no drama in the air. I sighed silently in relief.

"Moira just called," Jeffrey informed me as if I didn't know. "She needs me to go over to the head office and pick up the transfer papers for the purchase of the business. It seems she wants to go over them."

I felt like pointing out that Moira had legs and she could have gone herself to the head office, but I bit back the retort. At least, there was visible progress in the situation and it would hardly help if I made more demands on him now. Besides, he had spent the whole afternoon with me, and Moira hadn't even called once.

"Well, you better go then," I said, thinking ahead to the phone call with my mother.

Jeffrey picked up his jacket and kissed me goodbye. "I'll call you."

As soon as he was out the door, I raced for the phone and dialled London.

***

The following day, I met with Ping for lunch at a local restaurant close to my flat. It was a favourite with me, not only for the wonderful local cuisine, but because it was affordable, and Ping was my guest. Network marketing was a people business and entertainment of one's own colleagues was sometimes necessary. A team leader always needed to show they were successful in the business even if this was not the case. It was imperative to keep team members motivated by showing a confident and prosperous persona.

I wished to discuss with Ping her reason for wanting to drop out and to reassure her I was now back in Taipei for the long term and would work together with her to build up her team. We were in deep discussion, and I was outlining my plan of action for her business, when all of a sudden I noticed she was no longer listening. "Ping," I said, "are you okay?"

The look on her face had changed from that of a focused businesswoman to one of a lovesick teenager, and the hair at the back of my neck stood on end when she grinned from ear to ear and called out, "Mike! What a lovely surprise."

"Ladies, fancy running into you here."

When I looked up at him, I wasn't prepared for the feeling of attraction that hit me like a tidal wave. I felt mortified and couldn't understand why I still found him so overwhelmingly sexy when he had rejected me outright. Not only this, but I was supposed to be in love with Jeffrey.

Now, to my horror, Ping was inviting the man to join us. "Ping," I intervened, "I'm sure Mike is very busy."

Mike gave me a devilish smile that set my heart thumping and said, "In fact, I came here to meet with a colleague, but he cancelled at the last minute so I have time to join you ladies for coffee."

Ping was over the moon and swept aside the paperwork I had earlier spread across the table for our discussion. "Please, sit," she invited and gave him one of her goofy smiles while I wished I could wipe it off by slapping her on the back of the head.

Mike took a seat and ordered coffees all around. Of course, as usual, the waitress dropped everything and came to take our order the minute she saw him sitting at the table. I really felt like screaming at his smug head.

"I hope coffee's okay?" he asked.

Ping answered for both of us. "Of course. We just finished a business lunch and were discussing some strategies, so coffee is perfect."

I managed a smile in Mike's general direction but didn't want to look into his all-knowing, all-seeing eyes.

"I heard you were in London for a while, Sarah," said the devil. Yes, he was a devil! I fumed as I looked around for that ever-elusive ashtray, but I couldn't find one. I felt my temper rise and wished I could pour hot coffee over his head. Unfortunately, it hadn't yet arrived. So I forced myself to look in his direction and kept my gaze on a point somewhere between his eyebrows.

"Yes, I was there on a short business trip," I managed to reply, cool as a cucumber. "I had to look in on my team."

"I hope everything was in order. You know, no lost vitamins or any other items." His eyes mocked me, and I could feel them enjoying my discomfort even though I wasn't looking directly into them.

This is it! How dared he bait me in front of Ping, knowing I couldn't very well tell him to go to hell. He was, of course, referring to the shoes and jacket he'd couriered over the day after our stormy encounter.

"Everything was just fine, thank you," I responded with a forced smile, and the look he gave me told me he didn't believe me one bit.

So he was going to make me pay for having left him standing in the middle of the road on a cold night. Well, he could stew on it for the rest of his life for all I cared. As for Monica's suggestion that he had feelings for me, I was now sure this wasn't the case. Mr Ego had been gratified when I so stupidly threw myself at him, and his pride wounded when I bolted from his place without my shoes. Perhaps, he had been expecting me to beg. *Yeah, when hell freezes over.* I was willing to bet anything no woman had ever walked out on the great Mike Connor. No woman, that is, except his ex-fiancée. *Hurrah for Gloria!*

The coffee arrived, and Ping chattered away happily about Taipei, her family and friends, the business, and the state of the world in general. This gave me some respite from having to make conversation with the devil, and I took the opportunity to observe him. Today he looked drop-dead gorgeous in a light wool suit in charcoal grey with a white shirt that complemented the whiteness of his teeth. He wore a yellow silk tie, dotted with a pattern of small red *fleur de lys*. Conservative, but very sexy.

While Ping talked on, Mike stole a glance or two my way, making me wish I could slap the smug look off his face. In fact, I couldn't wait until our coffees were finished so he would leave. Fortunately, he finished his first and stood up, much to my relief.

"Ladies, I have to run to my next meeting, but it's been a pleasure. Ping," he turned his devastating smile toward the lovesick teenager she had become, "wonderful seeing you again and thank you for your company." Then he turned to me, and he wasn't smiling this time. "Sarah, I'm sure we'll be seeing each other soon."

Not if I can help it. I nodded casually, and he said his goodbyes and left.

"Wow, Sarah. He's so sexy!" Ping declared, stars in her eyes.

I couldn't believe it. It was obvious Gloria was the only woman in the universe who had managed to maintain her immunity to the devil. Three more hurrahs for the very clever Gloria! "Come on, Ping," I said, suddenly feeling exhausted, "it's getting late and I have another appointment. Shall we finish this tomorrow morning?"

She agreed, and we arranged to meet for coffee at Starbucks. On the way out, I asked the waitress for the bill and was surprised when I was informed, "The gentleman paid the account in full when he left the restaurant." *Grrrrr!*

CHAPTER 14

I tossed and turned that night and finally gave up trying to sleep altogether. Sitting up in bed, I flipped on the bedside lamp with the intention of reading something that would hopefully make me sleepy. Wrong! It seemed with every line I managed to read, a thought of Mike Connor popped into my mind. In the end, I gave up and made myself a cup of chamomile tea while I tried to sort out the muddle of thoughts inside my head.

It still didn't sit easy with me that Mike had paid for the lunch with Ping. I asked myself if the reason he paid was because I had picked up the tab for his lunch when we'd been working on my so-called project, and now he was returning the courtesy—or was it because he knew I was hard up? I rather hoped it was the former reason, but my intuition told me it was the latter. Who was I kidding? Mike had seen the way I lived, I thought with humiliation. Who wouldn't notice the old, rickety building without a lift, the kitchen bare of cupboards, the rusty fridge, and the neighbourhood rats scuttling across my rooftop terrace? On top of all this, I could only wonder what Rosepurple may have told him about me back in London. If she'd let him in on the Maggie Day situation, she was bound to have informed him on whatever else he wanted to know.

My mother knew about my financial hardship and had tried to help, but I'd been too proud to accept. I wanted to prove to her that I could do it on my own. *Fat chance!* I quickly sank into a negative state of mind and didn't like it one bit.

It suddenly occurred to me it was possible Rosepurple had let slip about my money situation to Mike and expressed her concern for me. And it seemed likely Mike had paid for the lunch as a gesture of kindness, and perhaps to let me know he was a friend despite what had transpired between us in London. Yes, this had to be the reason he had paid. As for London, the thought of that night still had the power to bring colour to my face and I felt my cheeks burning red hot.

Mike had admitted to wanting me, but not on the rebound. Yet he'd never made clear exactly what it was he wanted from me, assuming I wasn't on the rebound. Lately, this thought had started to haunt me day and night—even when I was with Jeffrey, which led me to wonder if I had done the right thing by returning to Taiwan.

In regards to Jeffrey, I wondered if I could really trust that he was going to break it off with Moira. For the first time, and much to my surprise, I acknowledged I wasn't sure if I truly wanted him to break it off at all. Now that my long awaited goal was close to becoming a reality, I didn't seem to want it anymore. Surely, this wasn't true, I argued with myself. After all, I had been waiting for this moment for a long time. Of course I wanted to be with Jeffrey! Then again, why did Mike keep intruding into my thoughts?

Frustrated and exhausted, I gave up examining my disturbing feelings and blamed them as a result of being on the rebound. Yes, that was it. I grasped at the thought quickly like a drowning man would grab desperately for a lifesaver. I had been so upset with Jeffrey lately that I had allowed myself to be charmed by the enigmatic Mr Connor. This was the reason, I sighed with relief. Why didn't I think of it before? Mike Connor was a sexy and attractive man—one no woman could resist; and I'd simply allowed myself to fall for his charm in order to block out thoughts of Jeffrey. Thank God this was all there was to it, and that I wasn't actually falling in love with the man. It had simply been a matter of rebound feelings after all.

Now, I could really get some sleep. I had a busy morning ahead of me with Ping, and in the afternoon I would be seeing Jeffrey. Dear Jeffrey, who was going to break it off with Moira in order to be with me.

I lay back in bed and switched off the lamp, a smile on my face as I thought of him while I fell asleep. Soon, all was peaceful again.

***

"What do you mean you can't stay?" I exclaimed, pacing up and down across the rooftop terrace with the afternoon sun shining down upon me. The pleasant warmth it cast escaped my notice as I was only aware of my mounting anger.

Jeffrey leaned against the balustrade and watched me with irritation in his eyes. "I can't stay, Sarah. I'm sorry, but the group in Tainan is far too important to be left on their own. My bus leaves in two hours, and I have to go home and pack."

"Why can't Moira go by herself?" I was close to a rage attack. This could not be happening again!

Jeffrey sighed with exasperation. "Because if she's going to sell her half of the business to me, I'm the one who needs to connect with the group. The Tainan group belongs to her, as you probably know."

"Okay," I said, suddenly inspired by an idea. "Then, I'll come with you. Ping has contacts in Tainan that she's been wanting me to talk to."

"I'm afraid this won't work, either. Moira's coming with me."

My anger bubbled over. "But you said it was going to be your group and you needed to connect with them. What game are you playing at, Jeffrey?"

"You just don't get it, do you?" He scowled at me. "You really don't get it! I discussed this with you a hundred times, and you still think this is one big holiday."

I felt like crying, and at the same time I wanted to lash out at him, but what was the point? All he cared about was the business. Even though he'd said he loved me, his actions certainly didn't match his words.

"If you're truly buying Moira's half of the business, I don't see why she needs to go along with you on this trip. You've gone with her a hundred times before and they all know you down there," I managed to say calmly. "If you mean it that we're going to be together, there shouldn't be a problem in my coming with you now. I intend to work while there, too, you know. I wasn't going to come along just for the pleasure of it."

Jeffrey was obviously not happy with my reasoning and he flashed me a look of annoyance. "I don't think you understand this business, Sarah; and you really need to think on this if you're serious about growing a large team in the future," he explained as if talking to a child. "Moira's coming along to inform her team that I'll be taking over. I don't want to discuss this further. This is my team, not yours. Besides, you'd be better employed working on your own lagging team right here in Taipei."

I was speechless and did everything in my power not to let my jaw drop wide open. He was talking to me as a boss would talk to an employee rather than to someone he supposedly loved.

Jeffrey must have seen the wounded look on my face and now spoke more softly, "Sarah, please give me a little more time. I'm doing this for the two of us."

I saw the sense in what he said but still couldn't help feeling upset. I knew full well that Moira didn't need to be with him on the trip. This was just her way of manipulating the situation. She'd done it so many times in the past, so why stop now?

I shook my head, feeling helpless. "I still don't see—"

Jeffrey interrupted me. "You know what you are?" he declared in a harsh tone, his eyes flashing fire. "You're selfish! I told you I loved you, and even paid your flight and rent so you could come back to be with me, but you still want more! You're just as bad as Moira, you know." He paused to take a deep breath and then his eyes pinned me with derision. "Frankly, I don't see the point in breaking off one bad relationship only to enter into another." He strode across the terrace and turned at the sliding door leading to the lounge. "I'll be back in a couple of weeks. In the meantime, you better figure out whether you really want to be with me or not." With that, he was gone.

I heard him slam out of the flat, and only then did I allow my tears to flow.

***

A whole week passed since Jeffrey's departure and I dragged myself to my appointments, working with different members of my team. I worked long and hard and came home late at night to my small flat only to collapse on the bed, sinking into a deep sleep that thankfully saved me from having to think about my situation for a few hours.

Jeffrey didn't call nor did he email. I tried to contact Monica in Hong Kong to fill her in on the latest, but her assistant informed me she was away in China on business. Disappointed, I decided there was no point in calling her over there as she was bound to be too busy to talk.

Another couple of days went by and still no word from Jeffrey. I was desperate to talk to someone. Anyone!

I didn't have friends in Taipei and I couldn't very well unburden myself on members of my team. Contacting Rosepurple was out of the question, too. My mother had been at me from the beginning to get rid of Jeffrey; and after she met Mike, all she ever talked about was how nice he was and what a pity I didn't go for someone like him. Oh, God! Even my own mother was in league with the devil.

Late one night, as I watched a DVD on my laptop, the thought struck me that I was leading a lonely and miserable life in Taipei with nothing to show for it. I had no friends, no family and, it seemed, no boyfriend. I didn't socialise with team members and there was no question of dating since I was supposedly going out with Jeffrey— *supposedly* being the operative word. In fact, in all of the time that I had been living in Taipei I'd only gone out socially with him twice— that is, without him answering his constantly ringing mobile phone.

On the occasions when I did go out with him, it was always for a quick dinner in case Moira became suspicious as to his whereabouts and started calling all his team members in order to locate him. This, of course, embarrassed him; something Jeffrey could not possibly allow. Therefore, we mainly saw each other when we met at my flat, assuming we had time to spare in between appointments.

Even if Moira hadn't been the issue, Jeffrey often worked so late that he didn't get home until the early hours of the morning. The Chinese did business pretty much around the clock, and he had to accommodate them. As a result, I was alone most nights, but even if I had been fortunate enough to have someone with whom to go out, I couldn't really afford to do it since my financial situation was very tight. Therefore, I usually stayed in reading or watching a DVD and cooking a lonely dinner—all the while thinking that being involved with Jeffrey meant snatching a few visits here and there for quick sex in between appointments. This was definitely not my idea of a relationship.

Jeffrey said he loved me but rarely showed it. He certainly didn't go out of his way to make time for me, not with Moira still in his life and his business appointments becoming more time consuming as his team grew from strength to strength. So I asked myself why I was waiting for a man who didn't seem to have any time for me at all.

When I'd gone back to London, I had seriously considered staying on, and would have, if it had not been for Jeffrey's email, telling me he loved me and asking me to come back. Now, I wondered if I'd made the right choice.

Even if Jeffrey managed to break it off with Moira, the kind of life he offered had no appeal for me. He was often gone after breakfast only to return at two or three in the morning, and he worked seven days a week. Did I really want to be involved in such a relationship? At least, Moira saw him more frequently because she co-owned the business with him so they often attended appointments together; whereas, if I was with him, I wouldn't be attending his meetings. My team was separate from his. He had his franchise and I had mine. Our paths wouldn't cross very often.

But I loved him, my heart wailed. Wasn't love supposed to be tolerant and understanding? It wasn't just about passion and excitement. I sighed, despondent and no closer to a better feeling about my current situation. When I looked down at my computer screen, I realised I had missed the whole movie so I shut down the laptop with yet another sigh. I was too tired to think anymore; only sleep would bring relief.

Another five days elapsed and still no word from Jeffrey. By this time, I became worried and finally gave in and called him. His mobile rang out and went straight into voicemail. I left him a message. When another two days passed without word from him, I could only assume two things: he was either still angry and didn't want to talk to me or Moira had deleted my message. She had done it before and I had no doubt she would do it again. In the end, I figured Jeffrey would be back in Taipei soon and I could wait until his return.

When yet another week elapsed, however, and there was still no word, I started to panic. Jeffrey had said he'd be back in a couple of weeks, and now it had been three weeks since I'd last seen him. I couldn't accept that he was simply ignoring me on purpose, so I assumed something terrible must have happened to him. A sudden vision of a mangled Jeffrey, lying dead by the side of a Taiwanese highway, flashed into my mind. The way people drove in this country was horrifying, and I shook my head to clear away the awful image.

I felt helpless because I didn't know where to turn. I didn't want to call him again in case he thought I was pestering him. So it was rather fortunate when I met with Ping and she happened to have news of him.

We were having coffee after a particularly long appointment one afternoon when she brought up the subject without knowing how it would impact me.

"It's a shame you couldn't go to Tainan with Jeffrey, Sarah," she remarked while sipping her coffee. "My cousin lives there, as you know, and she has many friends from university. I think it would've been great if you had been able to go down to meet them all."

I was stunned but thankfully able to speak. "I wanted to," I explained, hiding my annoyance with Jeffrey, "but he said he was going to be really busy with his own team and wouldn't be able to spend time with me if I needed someone to translate into Chinese." I had to lie about this; after all, I couldn't very well tell Ping the truth as to why I didn't go to Tainan.

"Oh," Ping sounded confused, "but didn't you know? Moira knows my cousin, and she and Jeffrey got together with her and signed her up plus a whole bunch of her friends. This is why they delayed their return to Taipei. They're now working with my cousin's team."

Now, it was my turn to be confused and shocked at the same time. "But why didn't Jeffrey call me? The new people are supposed to be part of our team."

Ping nodded thoughtfully. "True."

"So surely, it's my responsibility to be there doing the training with them," I reasoned while I kept indignation from creeping into my voice.

Ping gave me a blank look. "Maybe they thought since they were already in Tainan, they may as well save you the trouble of travelling," she suggested.

I nodded with half a smile and finished my coffee in silence. Then, I made the excuse of another appointment to get away before I showed my true feelings and embarrassed myself in front of her by going into a full rage.

How dared Jeffrey take matters into his own hands? This was my team and I had every right to be in Tainan working with them. He hadn't even called me to let me know. It was obvious he was happy to go on working with Moira and not with me. And to top it all off, it seemed he was now undermining me. This was unacceptable!

I thought I was going to explode with anger; but instead, I felt a deep hurt that knew no bounds and the realisation that Jeffrey had no intention of breaking up with Moira suddenly hit me. I sighed in desperation, wondering why he had wanted me back in Taiwan when he was acting like he didn't love me at all.

Then, it struck me. Perhaps, he only wanted me here in order to keep my own team going. After all, I had the trust of all my members; plus a percentage of everything the team made went to him, being the senior team leader of the whole business. This was how the business worked. The senior leaders nurtured the junior leaders, and as long as the junior leaders kept their teams in profit, the senior leaders benefited every step of the way.

I felt devastated. If all Jeffrey wanted from me was to have an enthusiastic team leader, one who would also provide him with a bit of sex on the side, then he had snagged me all the way in—hook, line and sinker—and I hadn't even seen it coming. Add to this the prospect of yet another lonely evening in Taipei ahead of me, and I wanted to cry. In fact, I was so close to breaking down that I thought the unthinkable; and before I had a chance to change my mind, I dialled Mike Connor's number at the bank. When he answered, I swallowed my pride and invited him over for dinner at my place.

CHAPTER 15

I didn't even want to understand why I invited Mike Connor to dinner, let alone at my place. The motivation behind it reeked of desperation. There was no denying I was starved for company, and I no longer worried about my surroundings or what Mike might think of them. In the end, I guess this explained the reason for my invitation after all.

Mike's gesture of paying for the lunch with Ping had brought home to me the sad truth of my circumstances and I realised I had been kidding myself all this time about being financially free. I wasn't an entrepreneur travelling the world and building a huge business—I was struggling to make ends meet, and if it hadn't been for Jeffrey, I'd have never made the rent for the month.

At the same time, for someone who thought of herself as a free-spirited woman building a business empire, I led a very solitary existence while missing the cosmopolitan lifestyle of Hong Kong and London. I missed my friends, my mother, her cat, and much to my amazement, even the great Mike Connor.

He may be a smug womaniser, but at least he had substance. I was sure I could depend on him under any circumstances, unlike Jeffrey. Not only this, but Mike seemed to know his own mind. He didn't hang around in dead relationships simply because the other party constantly threatened to commit suicide. I imagined how he would've handled someone like Moira and was sure he would have packed her off back to Singapore in five minutes. Suddenly, the thought of Mike with Moira—or with any other woman for that matter—made me feel defensive or was it jealous?

Enough about Mike, I told myself, and let out a yelp when I noticed the time. The object of my thoughts would be arriving in two hours, and I had better get a move on.

I normally liked to cook for others and tonight was my big opportunity to do so. On my own, I usually dined on a bowl of noodles, pretty much like the locals. When I had guests, though, I enjoyed being creative and ensured I prepared a delicious meal. Of course, all the while I had lived in Taipei, I'd never had a guest except for the rooftop rats, and they weren't very picky. Mike, however, would be my first human guest, and I was excited at the prospect.

It was a warm April evening so I decided it would be lovely to eat out on the terrace surrounded by the sparkling city views with, hopefully, no extra furry guests. I intended to use a small trestle table for dining, which was currently covered with potted plants, and I had a couple of folding chairs that I usually used when sunning myself. Fortunately, they folded upright so they would do well enough for dining.

Due to the limited amount of equipment I had in my kitchen, I planned a simple menu that could be prepared in a wok, a steamer and rice cooker—all essential pieces of equipment in any Asian home, even one as poor as mine.

I intended to start with small steamed vegetable dumplings served with plum sauce and Chinese vinegar for dipping. This would be followed by three main dishes: Szechwan chicken, beef with bamboo shoots, and stir-fried local vegetables, all to be consumed with fragrant steamed rice. For dessert, I chose a selection of local fruits including lychees, mangoes and star fruit.

I worked frantically for over an hour, setting the table, defrosting the dumplings, and organising ingredients for the other dishes. I intended to stir-fry at the last minute along with steaming of the dumplings. So with time to spare, I had a long shower and then wondered what to wear.

I settled on a long flowing skirt in black cotton embroidered with various Chinese patterns in gold thread, and a silky sleeveless top of burnished gold with a scalloped collar. On my feet, I wore a pair of delicate black velvet sandals with subtle gold threading, which complemented the rest of the outfit. I then gathered my hair at the nape of my neck and secured it with a silk scarf of matching colour to my top. Finally, I completed the ensemble with a pair of dangling imitation antique earrings made of brass and set with small amethyst stones. I wore a minimum of make-up, just a dusting of powder and blush, plus mascara and a touch of coppery red lipstick.

Much later, while I was scrutinising my appearance, the security buzzer alerted me that my guest had arrived and with butterflies in my stomach, I let him in. It had been a while since I'd seen him and I found I was looking forward to it.

I opened the front door as he was coming up the stairs and it was all I could do not to let my mouth gape open. As usual, his magnetism hit me with such impact I felt colour rush to my face. Mike didn't seem to notice and kissed me lightly on the cheek when he reached me and handed me a bottle of white wine.

"How are you?" He greeted me with his sexy smile, making my legs turn to jelly.

"Fine," I uttered, quickly moving away from him to put the wine in the fridge until it was time for dinner. "I thought we might eat out on the terrace. It's such a balmy evening."

"Sounds perfect," he replied, appraising my outfit. "You look beautiful."

"Thank you." I felt tongue-tied all of a sudden and couldn't think of anything else to say.

"Would you like help with anything?" Mike offered.

"No, thank you. Everything's under control. Just go on through to the terrace and I'll join you in a few minutes. There's cool mineral water on the table, so please help yourself." This would give me a little breathing room while I prepared the first of our dishes.

Mike gave me one of his dazzling smiles. "Call out if you need help."

I smiled in his general direction before turning to the stove to prepare our entrée and give my cheeks time to cool down. Mike looked gorgeous, and I tried to get my mind off his hip-hugging jeans and white cotton shirt, which accentuated an early spring tan.

When I went out on the terrace carrying the steamed dumplings for our starter course, I discovered he lit the candles I had earlier placed on the dining table. "Would you like me to open the wine now?" he asked as he helped me with the tray of dumplings.

"Thank you, yes. You'll find the bottle opener on the bench."

He went inside while I arranged the dumplings and made sure all other utensils were in place before he returned to pour the wine.

"Cheers," he said, raising his glass. "To a lovely dinner."

I laughed. "But you haven't even tasted it yet."

"Never mind. I know you made it with care and went to a lot of trouble with it, so I'm sure it's going to be wonderful."

I was touched by his words and thankful the only light around us came from the candles and the city skyline beyond, so he wouldn't be able to see me blush.

"Please, help yourself," I invited to cover my confusion at the feelings that ran rampant through my mind.

Mike served himself and waited for me to do likewise. "This looks great, Sarah. I didn't know you cooked local dishes." Then, he added, "Actually, I didn't know you cooked at all."

I sipped some of the wine and felt myself relax. "There's a lot you don't know about me." I felt daring all of a sudden.

He regarded me with a glint in his eyes. "Well, perhaps you'll give me the chance to learn more."

My heart skipped a beat and I quickly munched on one of the dumplings. Mike was already on his second.

"Very nice," he commented.

"I'm glad you like them."

"So what else do you do besides cooking?"

I felt hot under his gaze. "Nothing out of the ordinary really," I replied, trying to maintain a cool head. "I simply enjoy the company of good friends."

"And is that what I am—a good friend?" His voice was husky, a subtle smile touching his lips.

For an instant, an image of our night in London rose to my mind and I swallowed the wrong way, causing me to break into a coughing fit. Mike poured mineral water and pressed a glass into my hand.

"It seems I'm always rescuing you with water every time you choke on something," he remarked with amusement.

I nodded while I took a few sips and felt the cool liquid soothe my throat. "Thank you. It certainly seems that way."

He sipped his wine and regarded me thoughtfully. "Tell me, beautiful Sarah, *am* I a good friend?"

He was flirting unabashedly, and I blamed myself for having invited him over in the first place. "I … I guess so," I stammered like a village idiot.

He smiled knowingly and abruptly changed the subject. "I'll clear up while you get the next course ready."

I was puzzled but pleased he let me off the hook, and I sighed with relief when I headed for the kitchen to prepare the mains. Meanwhile, Mike cleared the dishes and took out clean bowls and a thermal container filled with steamed rice.

I had the stir-fried dishes ready in a few minutes and took them out in serving bowls. "I think I can cook pretty much anything in a wok. It's easy and quick," I remarked, still trying to figure out what was on his mind. First, he flirted with me and then became all practical and helpful around the kitchen. He had me blowing hot and cold, and the feeling was unsettling.

"Smells wonderful," he uttered, and once again helped to set the dishes on the table.

We sat down to eat and thankfully, the conversation flowed between us as if we were old friends. Mike didn't flirt anymore, and I was happy. At least, I thought so. In any case, I was able to enjoy his company without having to keep up my guard and the rest of the dinner was pretty much like the one we'd had in London, easy going with lots of laughter.

When we finished eating, I brewed Italian coffee to go with the fruit and we relaxed while enjoying the lights of the city skyline.

"So tell me the truth," Mike stated all of a sudden, "why did you invite me here tonight? I know it's not because you want a continuation to what happened between us in London."

The directness of his words left me speechless, and I was ashamed I had been so transparent. It was obvious he had guessed I felt lonely and this was the reason I'd invited him over.

As to what happened in London, he obviously hadn't forgotten about it. At this point, I wasn't sure whether to feel mortified or thrilled; and I didn't know what to say. At the same time, I realised I had to tell him something. He waited silently for me to speak, and I knew there was no longer any point in lying.

To my surprise, I found I genuinely liked him despite his rejection of me in London. I acknowledged that what he'd done had been for my own protection. Once I was able to get past my ego, I had to admit the way he handled the situation made me like him all the more. This led to my decision to be truthful with him once and for all.

"Okay, I confess. I was lonely," I answered, thankful the candles had burned down and my face was shadowed by the night. "But I don't want you to think I'm using you or anything like that. I think we can be friends, don't you? I simply wanted to invite you over for dinner, so I hope you don't mind."

His eyes seemed to see into my very soul even through the darkness of the evening. "I don't mind at all. Why should I? I'm dining with a desirable woman who's not only beautiful but smart, and she wants to be my friend," he paused before adding softly, "and I know I want to be hers."

I felt those pesky butterflies stirring inside my stomach and was grateful to be sitting down because I knew my legs wouldn't have supported me if I had been standing. I took a deep breath for courage and spoke. "Mike, there's something I want you to know. I mean, if we're truly friends, I want to share this with you." I felt uneasy but knew I had to get this out in the open.

Mike remained silent and waited for me to go on.

"It's about my relationship with Jeffrey," I remarked, and saw his jaw harden. I continued talking, "I've had a lot of time to think about things while he's been away in Tainan, and ... well ... I think maybe I ..." I found I couldn't finish what I wanted to say and threw him a look of helplessness.

"You think you made a mistake with him," Mike finished for me.

I nodded and saw his face soften.

"So what are you saying, Sarah?"

I held my breath for a moment and gathered my thoughts before I went on. "I guess I'm saying I'm re-evaluating my life and have certain decisions to make regarding the situation," I explained before plunging on with the rest. "I'm no longer sure Jeffrey's someone I want to be with. I think it's over between us and I don't know what I'm doing here in Taiwan, struggling with a business that doesn't show any signs of growth. Plus I miss my family and friends. So I think I should move on."

Mike stood and came around to my side of the table as he took my hand in his and gently pulled me to my feet. "Is this how you truly feel?"

I nodded, aware of the electricity between us.

"Then, I can finally say congratulations. I think you're doing the right thing."

I drew in my breath at his nearness and my lips parted naturally when I gazed deep into the dark green of his eyes. I was overcome by such a strong desire, I moved toward him unconsciously and then I was in his arms, with him kissing me hungrily, plundering my mouth with his—his tongue playing with mine in an erotic dance that had a language of its own.

I threw caution to the wind as my arms went around his neck, and I gave myself up to the pleasure of his touch, melting into him with abandon. His kiss became deeper and he picked me up in his arms as if I didn't weigh a thing and made his way toward my bedroom. Talk about romance novel stuff—and how did he know the way to my room? It must be a "rat" thing, I thought in the midst of growing passion.

Mike deposited me on the bed and looked my way through a haze of desire. "Do you know how much I want you?" he said thickly and took me in his arms once again.

I didn't need to respond; I simply luxuriated in the feel of his touch as he slipped off my blouse, leaving a trail of hot kisses along my neck and the top of my breasts. I moaned with pleasure and felt my fingers unhooking my bra, freeing my breasts for him. This time, it was Mike who groaned with desire as he teased my nipples with his mouth and caressed my body with searching hands. I helped him off with his shirt and explored his chest with my tongue, enjoying the effect I had on him. I felt like a hussy and loved it.

We kissed for a long time, tasting each other with wild pleasure, our bodies entwined together in a dance of passionate discovery.

"Make love to me," I heard my voice whisper in his ear, and then I felt his fingers easing me out of my skirt.

I watched as he slipped off his jeans, and I devoured his body with hungry eyes. I didn't think I could wait any longer. This was where I belonged and I wanted him with an urgency I'd never known before. I wanted to be a part of him and fuse my body with his so we could reach new heights of delight together.

"God, you're beautiful," he groaned against my ear, pulling off my scarf and freeing my hair as he ran his fingers through it. I rolled on top of him, kissing him and feeling his hardness against my pelvis—the only thing between us, our underwear, was about to be removed with urgent fingers.

My heart pounded and I was so overcome with desire, I just couldn't wait anymore. I straddled him and in a moment, he was deep inside me. We moved in unison and almost immediately climaxed together. The wonderful feeling of release made me moan louder than I ever had before, and it almost drowned the shrill sound that broke through our passion.

My head cleared suddenly, and I realised it was my telephone. I ignored the ringing. "Never mind," I whispered against his mouth. "The machine will pick it up."

Mike's hands were on my waist as he gently rolled me over onto my back. My legs wrapped themselves around his hips and I almost begged him to enter me, but I didn't need to. He was inside me once again, and my passion started to mount with every thrust of his body. I was at screaming point when a male voice called out, "Sarah, are you there? Please pick up."

Cold reality came crashing down around me when I heard Jeffrey's voice, loud and clear, coming out of the answering machine. Mike's body froze in the act and, from the tension coming from him, I knew he was listening intently. I closed my eyes and winced at the thought of what he might be thinking.

"I'm so sorry about our fight. I'll be by to see you tomorrow. I love you," Jeffrey's voice said and then he hung up.

I felt Mike's icy glare on my face even before I opened my own eyes. He rolled off me, his arms no longer enfolding my body. Instinctively, I sat up and pulled the bed sheet over my breasts.

"Don't bother," he uttered with anger in his voice. "I think I told you once before I didn't want a woman on the rebound."

He was up and dressing while I sat on the bed, unable to speak and feeling the misery of the moment. "You know, you really had me going—wanting to re-evaluate your life and saying it was all over with your boyfriend. Then making love or should I say having sex like some desperate woman who can't get enough. Did you think you were going to kill off a couple of hours until Jeffrey got back to the city to service you?"

His harsh words wounded me to the core. I wanted to make him understand that this wasn't the case. I wanted to tell him I had never expected a call from Jeffrey; that I truly thought it was all over; and that I wasn't sure I ever really loved him. I wanted Mike as I wanted no other man. I realised this and yearned desperately to tell him that it really had been lovemaking between us and not wanton sex. But nothing came out of my mouth and I simply sat on the bed looking even more miserable than before.

Mike obviously didn't see the play of emotions on my face nor did he sense the depth of my feelings. He merely seemed intent on taking his anger out on me even though I'd had no control over Jeffrey's phone call.

"I really thought you were smart, Sarah. But I think you still have a lot to learn; and whatever it is, don't expect me to be your teacher." He didn't wait for my response and made his way to the door.

I finally found my voice. "Mike!" I called out, crying on the inside for him to give me a chance to explain.

"Forget it! I don't want to listen to your excuses." He threw me a savage look. "And next time you're feeling lonely or horny, call someone who cares." Then, he left; slamming the door shut after him.

CHAPTER 16

I decided to meet Jeffrey at a local café. After the previous evening's terrible row with Mike, the last thing I needed was a repeat performance.

My whole body tingled at the thought of Mike's touch, and I found myself crying out for him with every cell of my being. Exhausted after a sleepless night spent reliving the evening with him—the wonderful dinner and companionable conversation; the passionate scene in my bedroom; and finally, our awful parting after Jeffrey's call, I couldn't focus on anything except the pain in my heart.

I was incensed and disappointed that Mike had not given me a chance to explain. He had simply assumed I was running back to Jeffrey without a thought about what I had said earlier. This made me wonder whether he usually gave up so easily. Whatever happened to our friendship? I coloured at the thought. What I'd had with him was not only friendship; that much was certain. Beyond this, I was not able to think because Jeffrey walked into the café and made his way over.

"Sorry I'm late." His appearance at my table brought me out of my reverie. I noticed he didn't attempt to kiss me—not that I cared any longer—and he sat down and ordered coffee for both of us without asking me what I wanted. "You look tired. Late night appointment?" he asked.

"Yes," I lied and hoped the heat rising to my face did not give me away. "How was Tainan?"

"Busy." He looked excited, and I felt like slapping him. It galled me, all of a sudden, that he didn't even bring up the situation regarding Ping's team. Surely, he knew she would have discussed it with me.

Our coffees arrived and we said nothing for a few moments while we sipped the hot drinks. The silence felt uncomfortable.

"Sarah," Jeffrey said after a while. "I'm sorry about the way we parted, and I want you to understand I'm doing this for the business and for us."

I raised a querying eyebrow. "Are you sure it's for us?" I wasn't convinced. "I think perhaps you're doing this for yourself *and* Moira."

He scowled. "Why can't you get past this?" He sounded impatient, and I held my irritation in check.

"It looks to me like you're building Moira's team because it's also your team, and this is all that matters to you," I stated in a matter-of-fact tone. "Frankly, I don't believe Moira's going to sell her half of the business to you. She's just playing games."

I noted he did not jump in to deny any of what I had said, and I felt the disappointment hit me like a tonne of bricks. It was obvious I was right. He had no intention of breaking it off with Moira, and even though my being with Jeffrey didn't seem to matter anymore, the fact that he had used me hurt me deeply.

"Sarah," Jeffrey sighed, "I need you to be patient. The thing with Moira is going to take time—"

"The time for patience is past," I interrupted him, my voice firm. "I know you've been building Ping's team in Tainan, and yet you didn't call me to join you there. You simply took over and worked with Moira."

He did not seem surprised at my outburst. "What was the point of getting you to come down? I knew you'd be busy with your team over here. And seeing as I was already there, I thought there was no point in dragging you away."

Now I felt my temper rise, but I kept it under control and spoke quietly. "You know what I think? I think you didn't want me there because Moira would have been upset, and you don't want to upset her, do you?"

"Why would I want to rock the boat?" he threw back, trying to reason with me. "I want her to sell me her half of the business."

"That's what you say," I retorted and didn't make an attempt to hide the doubt in my voice.

"Oh," remarked Jeffrey, clearly annoyed, "and what do *you* say?"

I looked straight into his baby blues and felt the sharp pain of betrayal in my heart. It was the pain of disappointment and lost dreams. "I say I don't believe you anymore. I say it's time you make a choice because I'm no longer prepared to wait for you. It's either her or me." I issued the ultimatum half-heartedly, without any intention of keeping him to it. However, he seemed to believe I was serious, and a look of anger flashed into his eyes.

"I don't respond to threats," he stated and gulped down the rest of his coffee. "And before you do anything crazy, I think you should take time out to think about this. I told you I'm prepared to be with you as soon as I deal with the Moira situation. But if this isn't good enough, you'll have to deal with things your own way."

I remained silent while he stood and dropped a few dollar notes on the table. "Think about this carefully, Sarah." He looked intently into my eyes. "Don't do anything you'll later regret." Then, he was gone.

What is the matter with these men? I thought with irritation. They were always walking out on me at restaurants or slamming their way out of my flat.

I watched Jeffrey go as my heart broke into little bits for the time I had wasted in the relationship. With him went my hopes and dreams of starting a family and all the time I had invested. I didn't believe for one minute that he was going to let Moira go; not so much because he loved her, but because it was too inconvenient to leave her. There was no point in his buying Moira's half of the business when he already owned it if he stayed on with her. This way, it wouldn't cost him a cent to keep the whole business intact.

I now wondered why I had ever contemplated marriage with a man who was married to a business and had another woman in tow. Come to think of it, I realised, yet again, Jeffrey had never once offered me marriage.

***

That evening I sat out on the terrace with a bowl of noodles for dinner. The city lights didn't look as exciting as when Mike had been with me.

Mike. What was he doing now? Probably dating another woman who was not on the rebound, I thought cynically, feeling outraged. The fact he hadn't given me a fair hearing really rankled. I wanted to ring him and explain my side of the story, but somehow I didn't think he would take the time to listen. He had been so angry with me that for a second I thought he was going to strike me.

Of course, I knew he would never do this, not even in the heat of the moment. Yet the look in his eyes when he'd told me off about Jeffrey had been unforgettable. It was like green fire—a passionate green that made me want to throw myself at him and beg him to make love to me again and again.

Stop it! What was the matter with me? I was supposed to be thinking about my situation with Jeffrey and my next move to save my dwindling business, not filling my head with thoughts of the intoxicating Mike Connor.

The telephone rang, making me jump up with hope. Perhaps, it was Mike calling, wanting to see how I was and regretting our argument.

I picked up on the second ring. "Hello."

"Thank God you're home." It was my mother, sounding agitated.

Momentarily, I forgot about Mike. "Mum, are you okay? You sound worried," I exclaimed with concern.

"I'm fine, dear. It's just that Maggie Day's come through again, and this is very disturbing news," Rosepurple informed me.

I sighed in relief. Was that all? My mother had exaggerated the information Jeffrey had given Maggie Day once before, so what could be any different now? I knew the last thing on Jeffrey's mind was to go to the UK to help one single girl when he had a huge team depending on him right here in Taiwan. "What now, Mother?"

"Really, Sarah," she chided me, "how can you be so unconcerned about all this?"

"About what? I don't even know what you're talking about." I then added with cynicism, "You're not calling to tell me Jeffrey's coming over to the UK to meet up with Maggie?"

"Worse than that, dear," my mother remarked in a serious tone. "He's putting both your UK and Taiwan teams directly under her."

"What!" My voice went up a few decibels while my cynicism dissolved abruptly. "What are you saying? This can't be true. How do you know?"

"Oh dear!" my mother uttered, sounding even more worried. "Sarah, are you going to be okay if I tell you what happened?"

I sat down on the floor before I fell down. I knew whatever Rosepurple had to say was not going to be pleasant. "Go ahead," I murmured into the phone, my heart in my mouth.

"Well, you know how Maggie isn't getting any help from her team leader, and this is why Jeffrey is helping her?"

"Yes," I remarked cautiously.

"Anyway, he emailed her just now and told her he's going to transfer a large number of people into her team because the team leader who's looking after them at present isn't quite working out. Then, he intends on coming to the UK to coach Maggie and ensure she knows how to support the new team."

"So what has this got to do with me?" I was puzzled. Besides, I knew that to take team members from one leader and transfer them to another was illegal. Still, I wondered who the team leader was that supposedly wasn't "quite working out." Then, I went cold all over. Surely, Jeffrey couldn't be referring to me!

"There's a girl—Ping Wang is her name," my mother continued as my heart jolted with fear. "Apparently, she's just signed up a whole bunch of people over there and she wants to place them under a cousin she has here in the UK. This way, she can travel between Taiwan and here, and grow the business with her cousin."

Rosepurple was totally unaware of the shock going through my body. "You mean Ping's team will be signed up under her cousin, who in turn is on Maggie Day's teamm and not mine?" I wanted to clarify this to be sure I understood correctly.

"That's right, dear. This is exactly what Jeffrey says in his email."

"But Maggie Day doesn't even exist!" I exclaimed.

"I know," my mother stated and went on, "but, Sarah, even though Maggie doesn't exist, her team leader in the UK is a real person with a legit business. By signing over all these people into Maggie's team, a percentage of the income this team generates will automatically revert to that leader, the real person, I mean."

I felt panic rise to my stomach and then spread all over my limbs, making me feel weak. What my mother said was correct. If someone dropped out of a team, it didn't matter because a percentage of the profits flowed upward; everyone getting a cut based on the size of their business unit. This was how multi-level marketing worked.

"But I thought you sent Jeffrey an email from Maggie, telling him she didn't want to be in the business anymore." I clutched at straws now, realising there was nothing I could do. It was all too late.

My mother concurred, "I did, which is why he decided to do this. He didn't want to lose her, you see. So this is his way of keeping her motivated to stay in the business. Apparently, he does it all the time, Sarah. If he wants to motivate someone to work the business, he'll place some people in their team so the person starts to make instant income, and this gets them excited and keeps them working even harder."

Rosepurple was an astute businesswoman, and though she didn't know much about the business, she hit the nail on the head with this observation. One of the things drummed into us with this kind of business was if you wanted to keep your team members motivated, you simply kept placing people under them. This way, not only did the team members earn income, but a percentage of that income came to the team leader. Therefore, it was in the team leader's interest to help the members of their team to generate more income by placing more people under them. This built a passive income stream and a solid foundation for the future.

I felt like my nerves were going to snap as I thought about what Jeffrey did. Then, I picked up on something my mother had just said. "What do you mean he does it all the time?" I was suddenly suspicious and thought of the number of people who had dropped out of my team while I'd been away; and at the time, this did not include Ping's people.

"I looked into his business reports where it shows all the different teams in his business units," my mother related. "And it seems from time to time a whole bunch of names jump from one team to another."

"But this is illegal, Mum." I was very alert now, my panic forgotten.

"Yes, but he's doing it, anyway. He's mainly doing it with the Chinese members. Apparently, they use their full Chinese names in one team and their English first names along with their Chinese surnames when they jump across to the other team. This way, they don't risk being caught out."

I couldn't believe it. To think Jeffrey would sink so low as to steal team members from one leader only to give them to another. The whole thing was ludicrous. "Are you sure about this?" I hoped against hope Rosepurple had it wrong.

"I checked it all out, Sarah. One day the person closes their account and the next, their name appears in another team with an English first name. They still use their real surname, however, and usually the same residential address."

Oh, my God! Jeffrey really was doing it, and getting away with it, too. He was stealing my people and weakening my business on purpose. This was a great way to get rid of me without having to break it off.

"And, dear," my mother added, "there's more."

What more could there be? My brain went into overdrive.

"I tracked down the names of all your team members and around seventy percent of them have changed teams over the last couple of months."

My heart plummeted to my feet and I broke out in a sweat. *That many?* My suspicion was confirmed—this was the proof I needed to finally convince me that I had been totally and completely duped. Jeffrey had been stealing team members from me, and it seems it began when we started having problems with our relationship.

It was true, then. He had no intention of leaving Moira. In fact, he probably never had; and now he was taking away my team members so I would give up and go home thinking I'd failed. I couldn't believe it. Not when all this time he had made it appear like he was interested in being with me. How could he do this? I felt sick to my stomach.

"Sarah, are you there, dear?"

"Tell me what I've lost, Mum," I uttered in a voice I didn't recognise as my own.

"Most members of your teams in Taiwan and the UK are gone. There are very few people left, I'm afraid. You do still have a small team in Hong Kong, though."

"Thanks." I felt defeated. It was all over. "I'll call you tomorrow. I have to think right now."

"Okay, dear. But are you going to be all right?" Her voice was full of concern.

"Yes, Mum. I'll be all right," I reassured her automatically and rang off.

I stayed sitting on the floor in deep thought and didn't even flinch when I saw a mouse scurry across the kitchen. It didn't matter. I was finished. I had put my trust in Jeffrey and he'd cheated me by taking away most of my business. And if it hadn't been for Rosepurple, I would've never found out he had been responsible for my loss. Instead, I would have concluded my team members had simply dropped out, no longer interested in working the business; and I would have felt like a failure.

How Jeffrey would have loved this! The gutless wonder hadn't even had the courage to break it off with me. He'd simply cleaned me out in the hope I would be fed up with failure and go home. This was his twisted idea of love.

What love? I asked myself. Finally, the bitter truth revealed itself to me. Jeffrey didn't love me and never had. He was a user and a thief, and I'd been a sucker all this time.

Monica had been right all along when she'd said he had it too easy with Moira in one corner doing the business and working alongside of him; and me in the other, ready to romp. The only part she hadn't picked up on was what a scoundrel Jeffrey turned out to be.

I closed my eyes and felt tears of humiliation escape from under my lids. Not only did I feel used, but I was now financially ruined.

CHAPTER 17

I shut down my laptop and sighed in despair. My income after the defection of most of my team was barely enough to buy groceries, let alone pay rent and bills. There was no way I could keep going if I stayed on in Taipei. In any case, there was no longer any point in staying, I thought with resignation. I certainly had no intention of seeing Jeffrey ever again.

After my conversation with Rosepurple, I spent another sleepless night going over what I learned. The fact Jeffrey kept leading me on, while at the same time calmly stealing my team members from under me, was something I couldn't accept. Once I checked out the information my mother emailed, however, I'd had to face the truth. My team members had been dropping off in a steady stream, only to reappear a day or two later in one of Jeffrey's other teams, with an English first name. Therefore, I could no longer deny the fact that I had been conned by the man who'd professed to love me.

Close to two years of hard work had simply gone down the drain because Jeffrey found it inconvenient to break up with Moira. To him, the business was everything and it was obviously so important, he was happy to let me go. At the back of my mind, I had probably always known that behind his go-getter attitude existed a cold and calculating streak, making him a man who would have no compunction in dropping me if I became too demanding. The only reason he still hung on to Moira was due to his greed for money and not because he cared for her as a sister. In my case, his motivation had been sex.

I shook my head with sadness and thought how extremely naïve

I'd been. Only now did it dawn on me that I was a diversion to him all along, and not the love of his life. I blamed myself for having misjudged him so; but most of all, I couldn't believe I'd been so blind to his true motives when all those around me had been able to see right through him.

In hindsight, it was easy to see the signs: his many excuses for not breaking if off with Moira; his unwillingness to make more time for me and always begging off at the last minute; and the list went on. I'd been the biggest fool of all! And to think I was stupid enough to try and have Mike romance Moira away from him. I could only thank God Jeffrey never got a whiff of my crazy plan because this would have been the worst humiliation of all time.

My thoughts now turned to Mike and how he must have laughed at my gullibility while at the same time playing the role of the other boyfriend. The one thing I couldn't yet figure out was why he'd agreed to go along with it in the first place. Surely, the man had better things to do than play a part for an innocent like me.

Anyway, what was the point of torturing myself about what Mike thought of me? Judging by the way we had parted, I very much doubted I would ever see him again. Besides, right now I had bigger problems to solve, such as what I was going to do with whatever was left of my business and, more importantly, where I was going to live. I knew I could always pack up and go back home to London, but I wasn't ready to give up just yet and let Jeffrey have the satisfaction of knowing he had driven me to failure.

As for his illegal actions, I briefly considered lodging a formal complaint with the company's head office, but saw no point in doing this for I would then have to explain how I had come by the information of my defecting team. In fact, I wouldn't put it past Jeffrey to turn things around and say that I had been spying on his side of the business, which was partly true, thanks to my mother. The last thing I wanted was to have legal problems with him. No, it was best to cut my losses and run. But run where? In any case, no matter where I ended up, I took comfort in the knowledge that although Jeffrey had succeeded in getting rid of me, his punishment would be living with Moira for the rest of his life—for I knew that as long as he wanted to keep his business intact, he could not afford to let her go. And Moira seemed happy to stay where she was. The two deserved each other.

It was a pity I hadn't realised this earlier. The other thing I hadn't realised until now was that Jeffrey's betrayal had hurt more in terms of losing most of my business than of losing his love. Sure, my ego had taken a beating, and I didn't relish the thought that I had been a mere diversion to him, but my heart was not breaking as much as I thought it would.

I derived a certain amount of strength from this knowledge and knew whatever happened in future, I would survive. It would take time, but I was sure I would come out of this and be the better for it. I had paid a high price for my naïveté, but I finally learned my lesson.

Now it was time to tie up loose ends; and before anything else, I knew I would have to start with Mike Connor. The thought of his thinking I'd gone back to Jeffrey at the drop of a hat was unthinkable, and though he would probably never want to see me again, it was important that I see him one last time and explain my side of the story if only to achieve closure. So before I could change my mind, I placed a call to him, not realising the lateness of the hour.

"Hello," answered a sleepy voice.

I panicked momentarily and considered hanging up on him, but I couldn't back out now. "Mike, it's Sarah. I'm sorry about the time. I didn't realise it was so late." I noticed it was past midnight, according to my watch.

"Sarah?" Mike sounded fully awake now. "Are you okay? Has something happened?"

I appreciated his concern, despite the fact he had been so harsh with me when we'd last parted. "I'm so sorry," I apologised again. "It's just that I need to see you tomorrow if you have a moment. There's something important I need to discuss with you, and then I promise I won't bother you anymore."

There was a pause at the other end of the line and I hoped he wasn't going to hang up on me. "Okay," he said, much to my relief. "Why don't you meet me at Medici's for lunch? It's close to my office. Say one o'clock?"

I agreed and wished him a good night. I was suddenly happy because I was going to see him in less than thirteen hours. But, considering the situation, why was I counting the hours before I saw Mike Connor?

***

Mike walked into the crowded restaurant and my heart did a flip. He was by far the most distinguished-looking man among the lunchtime crowd, making all the other successful business executives in the place pale into insignificance.

Today, he was wearing a navy blue suit and a pale blue shirt with a grey silk tie, which turned the green of his eyes to a deep emerald. I wondered why the man always managed to look so good, and it was all I could do to tell my body to shut up and control itself as flames of desire coursed through me.

He greeted me with a kiss on the cheek, and I was glad I had taken the trouble to dress in business attire, wearing a Chanel-style suit with a small houndstooth pattern. My hair was swept from my face with small black and gold hair clips and left loose at the back to brush against my shoulders. I wore minimal make-up, but enough to bring out my large hazel eyes. I knew I looked my best and was thankful for the small boost of confidence this inspired in me.

A waitress rushed over to take our order, not that this was a surprise, and once placed, Mike turned his attention to me. "Okay, what was so important that necessitated the late night call? Not missing me, I hope?" he teased, and it seemed his anger at our last meeting had never existed.

I smiled at him as I secretly wished I'd never called the meeting. Somehow, I didn't think the great Mike would care if I had lost my business or Jeffrey. He would only say, "I told you so" and wonder why I was wasting his valuable time.

Now, sitting opposite him in the busy restaurant, I found my tongue didn't work, and the amused and expectant look in his eyes did nothing to reassure me.

"Sarah?" he prompted.

Thankfully, out of nowhere, the waitress arrived with our Pellegrino water, and I wanted to kiss the girl. While she poured our drinks and stole furtive glances in Mike's direction, I had time to compose myself and get my tongue working.

"Cheers." Mike raised his glass to me, and I had the feeling he was fully aware of my discomfort. Perhaps, he thought this was payback time.

"Cheers," I returned, and took a few sips of the cool, refreshing water. "Mike," I plunged ahead, despite the amusement in his eyes, which made me feel like a young student explaining to the headmaster why she was in trouble. My tongue seemed to get stuck on his name, so I tried again. "Mike …um … there are two things, really. First, I want to clear up our misunderstanding of the other evening," I stated, feeling a hot flush rush to my face but ignoring it. "Second, I want to let you know that I lost my business," I blurted out, giving him a furtive glance.

Mike's look of amusement turned to one of concern. "What happened to the business?"

I experience sudden disappointment. He hadn't even asked me to clear up what had happened between us. I felt the hurt in my heart, but instead of crying out with the agony of my pain, I remained calm and replied, "Jeffrey … Well, it's complicated, but to cut a long story short, Jeffrey transferred members of my teams in the UK and Taiwan to his other teams. So I'm now left with a very small group in Hong Kong."

"I'm sorry to hear it." His tone sounded serious, but he didn't look surprised. He reached for my hand and held it in the comfort of his own. "Edna emailed and told me everything."

For a moment, I didn't know what he was talking about, and then it clicked. Edna was Rosepurple. How long had my mother been corresponding with him? I didn't know how to react to this piece of news. I knew she had been charmed off her feet when she'd first met him, but to keep corresponding with him … It was all too much.

Mike seemed to read my thoughts. "Don't think badly of your mother. She loves you and has been really concerned lately. So she asked me to keep an eye on you."

I almost spit out the water I was sipping. "Well, thank you, Mum, for appointing Mike Connor as my keeper," I declared sarcastically with something of my old spirit.

"Don't be upset. You must admit she was right about Jeffrey."

Why did he always have a point? I thought, feeling vexed. "How long have you known?"

"I've known all along, since Edna told me about the Maggie Day thing."

Our first course arrived and I bit back my tongue until I composed myself. My temper had a way of getting out of control much too easily these days, and the last thing I wanted was to start an argument with him. "You knew the night you came over for dinner?"

I threw him a suspicious look.

"Yes."

Oh, God! "So you only came over because you felt sorry for me!" I sounded like I was accusing him. But let's face it, I *was* accusing him.

Mike gave me a sharp look. "Sarah, let's get one thing straight. I don't accept dinner invitations because I feel sorry for someone. I just wasn't sure whether Edna had told you anything that night, and I wanted to be with you in case you wanted to talk about it. That's what friends are for. When you didn't bring up the subject, I assumed you hadn't yet found out; and I wasn't about to tell you. Besides," he added, raising an eyebrow, "you wouldn't have believed me."

He was right, of course. If he'd said anything about the business at the time, I would have accused him of trying to discredit Jeffrey. "Okay, I accept that," I sighed resignedly. "But you didn't want my friendship, either." I blushed under his gaze. The pain of his rejection was reflected in my voice, but I couldn't help it. His eyes turned a deep, dark green, and I hoped I hadn't pushed him too far.

"You seem to forget you were on the rebound." His voice was soft, but firm; and I knew he was angry all of a sudden.

"That's not true! I couldn't help it if Jeffrey chose that very moment to call." My eyes implored him to believe me, but it didn't look like he was going to budge, although his eyes lost their look of anger and he was his old charming self again.

"Well, it doesn't matter now." He seemed to dismiss the events as if they had never taken place.

How could he do this when they had meant everything to me? I bristled, but stayed calm. I hoped the fact that he could sound so casual about the whole thing didn't mean he hadn't cared one way or another. Unless for him, it had merely been a "roll in the hay", a diversion—just like the diversion I had been for Jeffrey.

These charming bastards are all the same after all, I thought cynically, and found I wanted to run away and cry.

"So what are you going to do now?" Mike asked, ignoring the changing emotions he must have seen crossing my face.

"I'm not sure." I felt disheartened. "I simply wanted you to know you were right, and that I was wasting my time with the wrong person."

This time, his eyes registered surprise. "And why would you

want me to know this?"

I shrugged. "I don't know. Maybe, because you were the one who helped me out with my silly project, and I thought I should tell you," I answered, trying to keep the sadness out of my voice—sadness that wasn't about letting go of Jeffrey, but letting go of Mike. After today, I would probably never see him again, and suddenly the pain of it was too much to bear.

Mike gazed at me thoughtfully and as I lost myself in his eyes, I realised I loved him. The discovery caught me so unawares I felt my stomach wrench with agonising pain. How could this be? I thought, shocked at learning this new truth. I couldn't possibly fall in love with someone so quickly when I was supposed to be getting over my misguided love for Jeffrey. But my love for Jeffrey had been on the wane for a long time, even though I never knew it. Now, I wondered if I had ever really loved him in the first place or if I had simply fallen in love with the idea of loving someone.

Still, what was I thinking, falling in love with Mike the great? He was charming rat number one … a smug womaniser … a Lothario, as Rosepurple had called him—though this was before she'd met him and allowed herself to fall for his charm, just as I had done.

I became aware that Mike was speaking and I hadn't heard a word he'd said. All I knew was the feeling of wanting to crawl into his arms and stay there for the rest of my life. "I'm sorry," I apologised. "I was miles away. What did you say?"

"I asked if you're okay for money." I thought he sounded annoyed, but I listened as he went on. "As a friend, I'll be glad to tide you over until you decide what you're going to do."

I couldn't believe it. He was offering me money and calling himself a friend after what we'd shared. My heart couldn't take much more of this. He should be sweeping me into his arms, telling me he loved me and wanted to spend the rest of his life with me, and move to the country to start a family. He shouldn't be offering me money! But moving to the country and starting a family was something he'd wanted to do with Gloria, not me, I told myself glumly.

The waitress came to clear away our plates, and I noticed I'd hardly touched my food.

"Everything okay?" the girl asked me.

I smiled apologetically. "Yes. I guess I wasn't as hungry as I thought. I'll skip the next course and just have a cappuccino."

The girl nodded and then turned to Mike. "And for you, sir?"

"The entrée was delicious, thank you." Trust Mike to turn on the charm, I rolled my eyes. "But I'll do the same as my friend." *Friend, again?* "A cappuccino and some almond biscotti if you have them."

The girl wrote down the order and walked off.

"So are you okay for money?" Mike asked again.

"Yes, I'm okay." There was no way I was going to accept money from Mike Connor, not even if I were starving in the streets of Taipei and had to eat the rats that lived in my apartment building. Right now, I wanted to leave the restaurant and go home to think about my new discovery—my love for him. And to think I had him in front of my nose all along and hadn't discovered my feelings until it was too late. I'd been an even bigger and blinder fool than I'd thought.

We finished our coffees with general chitchat, and Mike glanced at his watch. "I'm so sorry, but I'm going to have to cut this short. I have a meeting in ten minutes," he informed me and signalled for the bill.

So this is it, I thought as my heart broke into little pieces. This is the end.

"Don't look so sad." Mike's voice broke into my thoughts, and he gave my hand a squeeze, sending me into bittersweet agony at his touch. "Remember, I'm here if you need anything. So keep in touch, okay?"

Maybe, when hell freezes over. I nodded and knew he would be the last person I'd ever call. He was merely being kind to me, a friend.

Mike paid the bill and we walked outside into the spring sunshine. "I'll be seeing you." He kissed my cheek and was gone before I could melt into him one last time.

CHAPTER 18

"**W**hy don't you come and stay with me for a while?" Monica suggested over the phone. She had recently returned from her business trip to China, much to my relief.

"But I don't want to impose—" I began.

"Don't be silly. You're my best friend," she insisted. "Besides, I'm hardly ever at home, especially now I have to catch up on all the work that piled up while I was away. Do say you'll come, Sarah. At least, you've got your Hong Kong team to work with."

She was right. My Hong Kong team was still intact, and it would be a pity if I abandoned them. If Monica was happy for me to stay awhile, I could work with my team and help it grow. A ray of hope cut through my depression at the thought and I felt my enthusiasm for the business return. "Okay," I cried excitedly. "I'll come, but only if you let me pay board and share expenses."

"Good God, honey, you're so independent." Monica laughed good-naturedly. "I'll tell you what; we share the expenses, but don't worry about the board. My bank pays for it."

All of a sudden, I couldn't wait to leave Taipei. "You have a deal," I replied cheerfully. Then, I discussed my possible arrival date, as yet to be confirmed, and rang off.

First, I wanted to meet with the few people left in my Taiwanese team in order to explain what had happened even though I was sure they, too, would soon defect. I couldn't really blame them. If I wasn't going to be around to look after them, there was no point in their working without a team leader. Jeffrey and the imaginary Maggie were welcome to whatever was left of my Taiwanese team.

Jeffrey! The thought of what he'd done stung deeply, and I wished

I could confront him with it. Common sense, however, told me to avoid a confrontation and simply leave the country quietly. Let him wonder what I was up to. Besides, I was finished with him and Moira; and the thought was so liberating that I couldn't wait to get on with the rest of my life. Then, my heart plummeted down to my feet as I remembered it would be a life without Mike.

My heart ached every time I thought of him. I still couldn't understand why I hadn't been able to recognise my love for him sooner. Ever since I'd met him, I'd been so preoccupied with my infatuation for Jeffrey that I had been unable to see true love standing right in front of me. I'd been so blind. What I felt for Mike was so very different from the feelings I'd had for Jeffrey.

Jeffrey had been an illusion, simply someone to rescue me from my loneliness. Mike was someone who had become a part of me, like a twin soul. He often sensed my thoughts and knew what I wanted to say; he had shown genuine concern for me; and he was on the same wavelength as me, even though I hadn't realised it until now.

Deep in my heart, I knew he was the one. The one for whom I'd been waiting, the elusive one who had been hidden from me because I'd been looking in all the wrong places. My soul resonated with his and I knew we were somehow connected. This felt like no other feeling I'd ever experienced with anyone else. I only knew with him, I was truly alive. Inside my being, I saw myself with him—making love, raising a family, laughing, and growing old together. With him, I knew I had found my other half.

Unfortunately, I identified this when it was all too late, when Mike decided he simply wanted to be a friend. I sighed, shaking my head to disperse the image of his face from my mind. I couldn't believe love could hit someone so hard. It had been building up within me slowly, like a silent volcano bubbles away under the surface until it shoots up in a huge explosion. Now, all that was left for me was devastation. It was obvious Mike didn't return my feelings.

I knew he was attracted to me. This fact was indisputable, and his lovemaking proved it beyond a shadow of a doubt. However, where true love was concerned … Well, this was something else altogether. After all, Mike had never mentioned love to me.

Despite this, he had always been in the background while I lived through my drama with Jeffrey. He played along with my charade and listened to my problems, and even tried to warn me about my folly.

But like a fool, I didn't take heed. Even so, he kept an eye on me, just as my mother requested of him—and I had to ask myself why he did all of this if he didn't care about me.

Perhaps, he did care just a little, I consoled myself with this thought while my heart went on aching. Mike had been very considerate of me when we'd last met, and he'd even offered financial assistance. However, he hadn't talked about his feelings toward me. He'd simply shown friendship.

Sadly, I could not see myself being a platonic friend when all I wanted was to be loved by him. It occurred to me how ironic it was that Mike and I had wanted the same thing in life—only we had each picked the wrong partner, a partner who had chosen business over love.

***

"It's great to have you back," Monica exclaimed as we watched the chauffeur deposit my luggage in the guest room of her apartment.

"It's good to be back," I replied, happy to be with someone who truly cared about me.

"Let's go make some coffee and you can tell me all about it," she suggested once she tipped the chauffeur and he departed.

I had arrived on an evening flight from Taipei and found Monica waiting at the airport, together with the chauffeur. It was bliss for my raw spirits to be suddenly pampered. Monica engulfed me in a big hug while the chauffeur retrieved my luggage and within a few moments, we were ensconced in the back of the limo and on our way to Monica's place.

It took me close to three weeks to finalise matters in Taipei and give up my flat before I flew to Hong Kong and my new life. During this time, I did not hear one word from Jeffrey or from Mike. I knew Jeffrey found out I discovered the role he'd played in taking my team members away from me. I made sure my last remaining colleagues knew what had happened, and I felt reassured when these few honest souls told me they would stop doing the business rather than defect to one of Jeffrey's other teams.

I learned from them that many stories had been circulating about the way Jeffrey ran his business, and it seemed this was not the first time he'd taken people away from team leaders with whom he no longer wished to work. I was not surprised to learn this and, once again, could not believe I had been so blind— not only about my feelings for him, but also about the way he operated his business. If it hadn't been for Rosepurple and the imaginary Maggie Day, I would never have known about Jeffrey's ruthlessness.

So, true to their word, the remaining team members closed their business units and sent an email to Jeffrey informing him of the fact. They told him what they thought about his lack of ethics and how they would no longer consider being in the business because of his treatment of me. When they later informed me of what they had done, I was touched by their loyalty. Jeffrey never replied to their email, but I was not surprised.

A couple of days before my departure from Taipei, I considered ringing Mike to let him know of my plans, but as I hadn't heard from him since our last meeting I decided with a heavy heart to let sleeping dogs lie. So as my plane climbed up in the sky and circled over Taipei before heading for Hong Kong, I sent a silent goodbye to my lost love and mentally closed that particular chapter of my life forever.

"Okay, so tell me all," Monica urged, handing me a mug of coffee.

We settled in her roomy lounge, talking and enjoying the nighttime view of the Hong Kong skyline from the big windows. "I already told you what my mother did," I declared, and Monica laughed.

"Rosepurple is just great. Remind me to use her services if I ever need info on a straying male."

I agreed my mother had done me a great service although I hadn't appreciated it at the time. I expressed this sentiment to Monica.

"The thing is," she commented, trying to comfort me, "at least, you found out and didn't waste even more time with Jeffrey, the super bastard."

Yes, I thought, feeling depressed, but I'd been too blind to recognise my love for Mike in the meantime, and so I lost him. Now, I felt as though my life was over. Of course, I didn't voice any of this to Monica. "Yes," I said instead, "at least I didn't waste more time with him."

"So did you let him have it?"

I gave her a wan smile. "Not quite. I simply packed up my things and left. If I'd said anything to him, it would've given him the satisfaction of seeing how much he hurt me and my business. I think being stuck with Moira for the rest of time is punishment enough for anybody."

Monica lit a cigarette. "You're right, of course. Better to let him wonder what became of you."

I frowned. "You know what hurts the most? It's not so much the fact things didn't work out, but that after the way he carried on, lying to me about his intentions of breaking it off with Moira, he didn't even have the courage to face me and tell me the truth. Instead, he went behind my back and stole my team away from me, all the while knowing this would ensure I'd leave Taiwan and be out of his life forever."

Monica sighed in disgust. "Don't waste your time thinking about him anymore. The man was a nasty piece of work from the beginning and unfortunately, he played with your feelings. At least, you can rest assured your intentions were honest," she observed.

"Not quite," I confessed to her surprise. "I wasn't honest about Moira, and I'm not proud of this at all. Much as she was manipulative and a weight around Jeffrey's neck, she didn't deserve what I did to her."

"Surely you're not blaming yourself for the way Jeffrey treats her?" Monica protested.

"No, I'm not. But I did play a part in that, Monica. I should've known better," I murmured.

"Okay, so you should've known better," Monica opined, dismissing my feelings of guilt. "But, Sarah, you thought you were in love with the guy and you believed him when he told you there was nothing between him and Moira. You were conned by him, for God's sake!"

While I appreciated the fact that she was trying to boost my spirits, I sighed dejectedly. "I know, but I still wish I hadn't played a part in hurting her," I remarked. "Not to mention involving other people along the way."

Monica threw me a knowing look. "You mean Mike, of course."

At the mention of his name, my heart started to ache and I wondered whether this was going to happen every time he was mentioned in future. "I don't know what Mike must've thought of me," I confided with a tone of sadness I didn't bother to hide.

"Well, don't worry about him. He's a big boy and can take care of himself." Monica dismissed whatever Mike's feelings might have been about the situation. "By the way, you didn't say whether you saw him before you left."

My throat went dry. "I … No, I didn't see him."

Monica regarded me with disbelief but didn't pursue the matter. "You look tired," she said kindly. "Why don't you go and get some sleep? I'm sure by tomorrow things will look better."

I smiled gratefully at her and did just that.

***

The next couple of months passed in a haze. Most of my waking time was spent working with my team, and I often went for days without seeing Monica. However, we made a point of leaving one free night a week to go out for dinner and catch up. During these times, we chatted about everything that was happening in our lives, everything except Mike Connor.

I constantly changed the subject when Monica mentioned anything about him, and she made it obvious she knew I was hiding something, but she couldn't make me disclose any information. I was very good at deflecting all conversation concerning Mike, and in the end she gave up.

Meanwhile, I managed to keep thoughts of him to a minimum while I threw myself into my work. I usually came home late at night and crashed out on my bed, often without having the energy to get undressed before I fell into an exhausted sleep. As the weeks progressed, I lost all hope of ever hearing from Mike and my heart ached with such intensity that many times I wanted to call him. Thankfully, I managed to control myself, albeit with great difficulty.

Eventually, working long hours and eating on the run began to take its toll on me. I lost weight and started to look somewhat peaky. Monica kept at me to cut back on my work and rest more, but I knew I couldn't afford the luxury. I had to make my business grow and show the world I wasn't going down without a fight. Even so, despite all my hard work, my team did not make much headway. Then, I started to notice several dropouts.

"He's at it again," I announced to Monica one evening over dinner. "Jeffrey's taking away my Hong Kong team. I don't know why he's being so vengeful when he's the one who's committing the crime; but he's doing all the same."

We were at the Hainanese restaurant where we had once run into Mike. I tried not to think about this while I furtively looked around in case he should suddenly make an appearance, but what were the chances?

Totally unaware of my thoughts, Monica sighed with exasperation. "Why do you put up with it? Report him!"

I shook my head at the futility of it all. "There's no point. His business is far too big for the company to take any action against him. Besides, he'll deny it. He knows how to cover his tracks." There was a tone of defeat in my voice, which hadn't been there in the past. "Anyway," I added, sounding tired, "maybe it's better this way. Who am I kidding to think I could keep the business going when I have Jeffrey sabotaging every move I make?"

Monica regarded me with concern. "I won't argue about that although it's not fair he should be allowed to get away with it. So what will you do now?"

I shrugged my shoulders. "I'll go home, I guess. Find a job and start all over again."

Monica said with sympathy in her voice, "I'm so sorry, Sarah. You worked so hard, and for what?"

I sipped my wine and shrugged again. "That's what you get when you're blinded by infatuation," I stated and saw her look of surprise. "Yes," I declared, "it was infatuation with Jeffrey after all. It was never love."

Her eyes widened with incredulity. "Well, knock me over with a feather! How do you know this all of a sudden? I thought you were head over heels for him."

I didn't feel I could explain anything right now without breaking into tears, so I changed the subject abruptly. "I plan to stay here another couple of months if you don't mind. I have to make some money for the airfare while I still have a team."

"Don't be silly. I can lend you the money any time you're ready to go," she offered.

I threw her a spirited look despite my heavy feeling. "No, but thank you. I got myself into this mess, and I'll get myself out of it."

She smiled. "Boy, are you stubborn or what?"

"I can't keep depending on other people, you know, much as I appreciate their help."

Monica seemed thoughtful for a moment, and then her eyes lit up. Surely, not another plan, I thought, seeing her look of excitement.

"I just remembered," she exclaimed. "There's a temp assignment in one of the departments at the bank. We need a data entry person for about three months for a particular project we're working on. Why don't you take it? It'll give you the extra cash you need."

I was relieved to hear good news for a change. "If you're offering, count me in. It would really help. Thank you."

With this settled, we talked about the assignment while we finished our wine, and then ordered coffee and dessert.

"I'm glad you're going to move on," Monica remarked. "I was beginning to worry about you. You're looking so tired these days, and you hardly ate anything tonight."

"I promise I'll look after myself from now on, Mother Monica," I returned in jest.

We laughed at this until suddenly, my smile froze on my face.

"What is it?" Monica uttered, noticing the way I looked. "Are you sick?"

"Mike." I barely whispered his name.

"Mike who?"

"Mike Connor, that's who!" I whispered savagely across the table. "He's just walked in with that woman …"

"Gina?"

"That's the one." I frowned. "What is it with him? Does he have a built-in radar that tracks us down wherever we happen to be?" Before Monica could respond, however, Mike was at our table, exuding sensual maleness in black pants and a casual black silk shirt. His eyes were greener than I remembered, and his smile brought a lump to my throat. I lowered my eyes, hoping he wouldn't see the hunger in them.

"Sarah, long time no hear," he said by way of greeting.

You can say that again. I wanted to run away but knew my legs would not even carry me as far as the exit door. Instead, I managed a lukewarm smile in his direction and hoped for the best.

Mike fortunately turned to Monica and kissed her cheek. "Great to see you."

Monica smiled, but her eyes took in my troubled expression, and this made me feel even more uncomfortable. "Likewise," she replied, but threw me a knowing look.

"I'm here with Gina," Mike stated, motioning for the woman to join in.

I noticed the sultry Gina didn't look too happy to see us. Another female with the hots for Mike Connor.

"Gina," Mike addressed her, "you remember my friends." Friends again! I winced mentally.

Gina managed to paste an acceptable smile on her face without cracking her make-up, I observed, feeling somewhat uncharitable toward her.

"Of course! Sarah and Monica, how are you?" She was wearing a sleeveless black dress that came just above the knee and clung to her in all the right places. Suddenly, I disliked her immensely.

"So how did it work out with the domestic agency?" Monica enquired, probably wondering why I was looking daggers at Gina.

"Great, thank you. I found a wonderful housekeeper." She smiled, showing her pearly whites, and I didn't think my dislike for her could get any stronger, but it did.

"So, Sarah, how's business?" Mike ignored my stony-faced look.

"Okay." I wasn't going to tell him what had happened to my so-called business, especially not in front of his ladylove.

"I ran into Ping a couple of weeks ago," Mike went on. "She told me you moved to Hong Kong for good."

Ping! That traitor who defected to Maggie Day's team! I fumed silently. She had certainly made sure Mike knew everything about me. Worst of all, it occurred to me that although Mike knew I left Taipei, he didn't bother to call. Why? *Because he doesn't care about you. That's why.* He had the delectable Gina to play with, so he would hardly bother with gullible little me.

"I decided to work with my team over here," I explained coldly, discouraging further conversation.

"Well, we'll leave you two ladies to your dessert." Mike obviously decided not to probe further, especially as a waiter arrived with our order. "We'll do lunch sometime, Sarah." He gave me one of his devastating smiles.

Yes, when the moon turns pink! "I'm sure." I managed a smile.

He said his good nights and guided the ravishing Gina toward their table with a hand on the small of her back.

"You're in love with him," Monica announced the minute he

was out of earshot, and a big smile spread across her face.

CHAPTER 19

"Okay," I conceded grudgingly when we returned from the restaurant and were lounging around in Monica's apartment, having a nightcap. "I admit it. I'm in love with Mike Connor." It sounded so incredible to my ears, but I was happy I could at last voice my feelings to someone I trusted.

Monica regarded me with a self-satisfied smile and not one bit of surprise. I was obviously predictable.

"In regards to your initial plan to play matchmaker with Mike and me," I spoke before she could say anything, "I'm sure even then you knew Jeffrey was the wrong person for me. If only I'd seen it myself." I sighed despondently. "In hindsight, I guess everything always makes sense and is crystal clear. What was I thinking, going on with this mad scheme to find Moira a boyfriend just to get Jeffrey for myself? Why couldn't I see he didn't even love me?"

"No need to beat yourself over the head now, Sarah. Let it go. Put it down to a bad experience and get on with your life," Monica advised.

I sighed again. "The point is how do I get on with my life? I've only just discovered my feelings for Mike, and you saw him with Gina tonight. It looks like they're an item." I still felt sick at the thought of this, especially when I remembered the sexy black dress Gina had been wearing at dinner.

Monica frowned. "I can't say I didn't wonder about him and Gina," she replied, looking at me with empathy. "And I don't know whether I should be telling you this, but in the banking community the talk is Mike relocated back to Hong Kong and that Gina is the reason for it."

I felt as if a knife was plunged into my chest. What chance did I have with him now? No wonder he had only wanted friendship from me. I felt depressed.

"I'm sorry, honey." Monica noticed the pain in my eyes. "This is only gossip, you know," she added encouragingly. "In truth, we don't really know what's going on between them. Remember that."

Well, I'm not likely to forget it! I thought desperately. I knew it wouldn't take long before Mike found someone irresistible. He was the kind of man who would never be without a partner.

I made an effort to push away the pain of losing him and gazed at Monica curiously. "How come you never made a play for him yourself? You once said he owed you a favour. What was that all about?"

Monica smiled. "I don't deny Mike's a gorgeous man and a wonderful catch, but we're too much alike in temperament, and we want different things. It would never have worked out. When he broke up with Gloria, he stayed with me for a while."

My eyes registered surprise.

"It's not what you think," Monica uttered. "Gloria took her time preparing for her job in New York so she stayed at their apartment until her departure. Mike thought it best if he was out of her way and bunked here until she left. Though he didn't show it, he was crushed, Sarah. His illusions about marriage and a family were destroyed by her ambition."

I was intent on what Monica said. This was a side of Mike I had never known. He was always so confident, sometimes even smug, so it never entered my mind that like most people he, too, had feelings. "You said you two were alike in temperament but didn't want the same things?" I wanted to know as much as possible.

"Yes, Mike's an ambitious man, and has every right to be. He's gifted at what he does and he'll always have a bright future. I'm ambitious, too, just like Gloria, and I'm not looking for marriage and a family—at least, not yet. But it seems to me Mike wants to settle down with the right person. I guess I always knew if I got together with him, I would've done exactly as Gloria did. So we stayed friends instead."

I was dying to know whether anything more than friendship had passed between Monica and Mike. After all, he would've been very vulnerable during his break up with Gloria, and Monica would have thought nothing of comforting a friend with something more than sympathy. She was a modern career woman and often got involved with no strings attached; but I couldn't bring myself to ask. Fortunately, she volunteered the information.

"I don't think Mike would've gone for someone like me, not even for comfort sex. I think he saw too much of Gloria in me. Besides, at the time, he was absolutely heartbroken."

I was secretly relieved Mike had never become involved with my best friend. I didn't think I would have been able to handle it. At the same time, I felt for his heartbreak. But now there was Gina. She might turn out to be the kind of girl with whom Mike would want to settle down. Most importantly, the talk about their being an item was an indication this could be the case.

Gina was younger than I by at least eight years, so having children wouldn't be a problem for her. While here I was, teetering on the brink of menopause, so what could I possibly offer him except hot flashes and the occasional panic attack? This was depressing beyond measure, and I had all the more reason to believe Mike had never really been interested in me as his mate for life. He'd probably acted on his temporary attraction for me and his male lust.

So Mike and Gina were an item! This was the gossip, Monica had said. And much to my despair, the evidence seemed to point in that direction, as I found out over the next few days when I commenced my temp assignment at Monica's bank. Everywhere I turned, I heard whispers about them. It was unbearable.

Mike's bank was a major competitor with Monica's and anything that happened in their small community was cause for talk. One morning, I overheard two women in the staff room discussing Mike, and I took my time getting myself a coffee. I couldn't resist listening in.

"I think he came back for her," one of the women said.

"Well, what do you expect? Gina's a knockout, the lucky woman. Just think, to be pursued by that hunk of a man," her companion replied with a star struck look in her eyes.

"You know, I've been here since the days when he split up with his then fiancée, and I can't get over the resemblance between the two women," the first woman commented in a conspiratorial manner.

"Poor man! Maybe, he never got over the break up. Do you

think …" Then, the women moved away and I was left with my heart in my mouth at the realisation that perhaps Mike never really did get over the break up with Gloria. If Gina reminded him of his former fiancée …

"Sarah, there you are!"

I almost spilled coffee down the front of my blouse when Daniel, my supervisor, walked into the room with a cheery look. "I want you to run over to Botticelli's and pick up a report from Graham. I need it now and he doesn't have time to bring it back himself. He's having lunch with a client."

Botticelli's was one of Hong Kong's premier Italian restaurants, and Graham was the big boss of my section. So I put down my coffee and left the building immediately. I found Graham within the restaurant's cool interior, having lunch with an elderly man.

He looked up and waved at me. "Over here, Sarah. Daniel said you'd be coming by," he stated and excused himself from his companion for a few moments. He handed me a big folder. "This is it. Thanks for running down to pick it up."

"No problem, Mr Irving." I took the folder from him and said goodbye. Then, as I turned to walk out, I saw Mike and Gina lunching at a discreet corner table. My first reaction was shock followed closely by horror. The last thing I wanted was for either of them to see me, so I held up the folder close to my face, hoping they wouldn't notice me, and I started to make my way out of the restaurant when I heard Mike call out my name.

Oh, no! I had no option but to look up and force a smile to my face as I made my way over to their table. I couldn't help but notice Gina's scowl at my approach and I suddenly wished myself over in Siberia. What I wouldn't give for teleporting.

"Fancy running into you here," Mike said, a genuine smile of pleasure on his face. "Why don't you join us? Have you had lunch yet?"

"No, but I have to race back to the office," I was pleased to explain, happy in the knowledge that I could make a hasty getaway without having to invent an excuse. "I came by to pick up a report," I added, noticing the hostility in Gina's glaring eyes.

"What are you doing picking up things from Graham Irving?" Mike asked in amused curiosity. "Don't tell me you signed him up."

I was momentarily puzzled. But of course! Mike didn't know I gave up my business and was now temping for Monica's bank. "I'm not doing the business anymore," I explained quickly, hoping he wouldn't ask any other questions. "I'm doing a short-term assignment for the bank and then I'm going back to the UK." This announcement was met with two reactions: surprise from Mike and delight from Gina.

"That's great!" Gina declared all of a sudden. "I bet you're looking forward to going back home. Too hot here." Now, she was all smiles.

I wanted to smash an ashtray over her pretty head, but we were in a non-smoking area so I simply said, "Yes, well, I'd better run. They're waiting for this report. Nice to see you both. Bye." I made my escape before Mike had a chance to say anything further, but not before I saw Gina's hand reach across the table to rest on his sleeve.

I practically ran out of the restaurant before tears of anguish spilled out of my eyes. So it was true. They really were an item.

***

"You have to tell him how you feel," Monica insisted over dinner that evening.

We were dining at a local Chinese restaurant around the corner from her apartment building, and I kept throwing anxious glances toward the door, hoping Mike did not take it into his head to dine at the same restaurant, especially if he brought Gina along. I didn't think I could handle another display of affection between them. In fact, I knew I couldn't. Just the thought of it made my tormented heart ache.

"Sarah, are you listening to me?" Monica snapped her fingers in front of my eyes. "I think it's time you tell him."

I had heard the first time around, but I was too shocked at her suggestion to answer straight away. Now, I replied, "Are you mad? I can't walk up to Mike Connor and tell him I love him! He'd laugh his head off, and then he'll regard me with a smug look and tell me he's not interested in me that way, but he's flattered I love him." Just the thought made my flesh crawl.

Monica seemed amused by my reaction. "You don't know this. Think for a moment. Why do you figure he helped you out in the first place?"

"Because he was bored?" I suggested, looking depressed. "You said so yourself that Mike was in for this sort of thing, so stop playing devil's advocate."

"I was only fooling you, remember? My ultimate goal was to get the two of you together," she reminded me. "Honestly, as if Mike would ever be involved in something so underhanded for no reason whatsoever. I told you he's a nice guy."

"Great!" I exclaimed. "So now you're telling me he consented to do something underhanded just to be near me. I can only cringe at the thought of what he must have thought of me in the first place—a silly woman who had to resort to subterfuge in order to get a man." I spoke with self-loathing.

Monica laughed. "You sound like a character out of a novel, you know that? So dramatic! You should loosen up. I genuinely think he has feelings for you, and you should give him a chance."

I suddenly felt annoyed. "All I know is he likes me as a friend, but that's not the point. He never gave me any indication he might have deeper feelings for me, and you just think I should go up to the man and blab all about my love for him? I would rather chew glass." I was desperate but glad to see I still had some pride left.

"Have it your own way," Monica sighed in exasperation. "But remember, you already let one chance slip by. Are you going to let this one go, too?"

"Monica, the man's in love with Gina. This is plain to see. You should've seen them at the restaurant, having an intimate lunch in a dark corner." My voice was full of pain, and for once I didn't try to hide it as Monica knew how I felt.

"You don't know this for sure. You only saw two people having lunch, that's all," Monica persisted.

"Yes, but the way Gina scowled at me and her reaching across the table to touch him, what does that say about her?"

"Forget Gina!" Monica admonished. "Just because she's jealous of you doesn't mean Mike loves her. This is the point I'm trying to make, dummy. You don't know how he feels about her—you only know that she doesn't like you being around him."

She had a point, and it gave me reason to hope, but I shrunk from the thought of having to reveal my feelings for him. What if I was right and he laughed at me and then went on to reject me in as gentle a way as possible? I knew I could never endure it. Besides, he probably wanted kids, and I was getting a little bit too long in the tooth for that sort of thing. No, forget it. I could never tell him. I would rather go home and suffer for my lost love in silence.

But what if I went home and gave up my one and only chance at happiness because I'd been too afraid to tell him how I felt? And if Mike really wanted kids, we could always adopt. I wanted to scream with frustration. There was only one thing to do in a situation such as this, and that was to drink as much wine as possible in the hope I would be unconscious for the rest of the evening. Of course, this was the childish way out, and I couldn't very well block Mike from my mind forever. Even an ocean of wine would never do the trick, as if that were even possible. God, I really had it bad.

CHAPTER 20

The end of my temp assignment was drawing near, and I now had enough funds saved to get myself back to the UK and start afresh. Since I had seen Mike lunching with Gina at Botticelli's, I kept busy trying not to think about him or Monica's suggestion that I should tell him about my feelings.

Despite my resolution to put him from my mind, however, I found thoughts of him haunting me during the day and creeping into my dreams at night. As a result, I worked even harder, hardly taking time out to eat, and I often didn't bother much with dinner, either.

Monica became worried at my behaviour. "You're running yourself into the ground," she chastised me in a serious tone. "You're losing heaps of weight, and you look tired all the time. You have to put a stop to this, Sarah!"

But how could I put a stop to love? I wondered. I couldn't just turn off my feelings; and disclosing them to Mike was not something I was prepared to do. I had toyed with the idea of telling him but since then, I'd run into him at restaurants I frequented or at industry functions; and every time Gina happened to be with him, either hanging off his arm or standing close by, whispering something in his ear. So in the end, I gave up on the idea. I had no doubt that before too long he would announce his upcoming marriage to her.

On the occasions I ran into him, Mike made an attempt to talk to me, but I managed to find a way to escape as quickly as was humanly possible. I figured if he wanted to talk, he knew where to find me. But he never called. Daily, I expected to hear of his marriage through office gossip, and I waited on tenterhooks.

It was now a well-known fact that Mike had relocated to Hong

Kong, but as to whether he did it for work reasons or to be with Gina remained to be seen, and people loved to speculate on this point.

Meanwhile, I repeatedly ran the thought in my mind that even if I rummaged up the courage to tell Mike of my feelings, I was sure I would have gotten one big rejection from him. This was something I would not be able to endure. Therefore, in self-preservation mode, I kept away from becoming involved in any talk about the popular couple; and when I finally completed my temp assignment, I started to make preparations to leave for home.

I booked my flight to London and telephoned my mother to let her know of my arrival date, and I took leave of my ex-team members in Hong Kong, disposing of the last of my vitamin stock through them. When all loose ends were tied up, I began to think about what I was going to do once I reached the UK.

"So what now?" Monica asked one evening when we returned to the apartment after having dinner out.

"I'm booked to fly out in three days' time, so there's really not that much left to do except my packing." My voice was matter-of-fact, but I knew I couldn't hide the pain from my friend.

Monica sighed. "Oh, Sarah, I just wish you would see him one last time to tell him you're leaving."

I rounded on her. "Why should I? He hasn't even called, and he knows I live here with you. He's obviously too busy with his new girlfriend." There was bitterness in my tone.

"Perhaps he thinks you don't want to see him," Monica protested. "We ran into him often enough during the past few weeks, and you always run off after the initial 'hello, how are you' stage."

I shrugged. "I can't help it, Monica. You saw the way Gina clings to him. It's like Mike's become her possession."

Monica frowned. "I still think you need to talk with him. I can swear he's still attracted to you, and I know he's been looking out for you. He's always been concerned about the situation with Jeffrey—you admitted this yourself. So don't you think you owe him a goodbye at the very least?"

I pondered on this for a moment. Perhaps, she was right. Mike may not love me, but he had certainly been decent where I was concerned, and he even offered help when I lost the business. The least I could do was let him know I was leaving.

"Okay," I agreed at length, "I'll tell him. As you say, it's the least I can do." When I saw the look of excitement in her eyes, I added, "But that's all I'm doing. I'm not going to tell him about my feelings. I'm just going to say goodbye to him."

Monica smiled, looking somewhat smug; and before I could ask her what was on her mind, the phone rang, and she began to talk at length with a business colleague. I left her to her own devices and turned in for the night, feeling rather excited. I was going to get to see Mike one last time, and I would engrave the moment in my memory as I had done with all the other moments I'd spent with him in the past.

***

I telephoned Mike the following morning and asked to see him. He didn't ask the reason but simply made a time for us to meet at a café near his office in the early afternoon.

A feeling of anticipation coursed through me, mixed with bittersweet pain. This was going to be the last time I saw the man I loved. To think I had come such a long way since the days when I believed myself in love with Jeffrey. What did I know then? I'd been silly to try to find Moira another man in order to get her to leave that rat. Instead, in the process, I fell for Mike, the other boyfriend, and now I felt like a different person. The Sarah of the past was gone and replaced by someone more mature—a woman who had been able to find and recognise a love she never knew existed, only to have to give it up because the man she loved was pursuing another woman.

How ironic the whole thing had turned out to be. I pursued Jeffrey when he was with Moira. Now, here was Mike with Gina. This time, however, I wasn't pursuing anybody. I had learned the hard way, and whatever life held for me, I would face the reality of it without the need to play any more games.

The most important thing I learned out of this painful experience was that a person couldn't change the feelings of another to suit their own desires. If a person didn't want to be with someone, nothing, absolutely nothing, could be done about it. I now acknowledged this, painful as it was.

Jeffrey had not wanted to be with me, despite his reassurances—and no matter to what lengths I'd gone to get him to leave Moira, I had been unsuccessful in my objective. If he truly wanted to be with me in the first place, I wouldn't have had to do anything about it because he would have simply dropped Moira without being asked. It was obvious now that Jeffrey had never felt love for me in any way.

The same thing applied to Mike. He was with Gina, and if gossip was anything to go by, they were an item. It seemed Gina reminded Mike of his lost love. According to Monica, Mike had wanted marriage and a family with Gloria, and now there was nothing to stop him from having this with Gina instead. The fact they had been seen together so often was a clear indication he had feelings for her and meant to marry her.

I felt the now familiar pain strike at my heart. I didn't want Mike to marry Gina. I wanted Mike to marry me! With this thought going through my mind, I made my way to the café to meet him at the appointed time and found him waiting for me when I entered. His smile made me want to weep along with my breaking heart.

"Thanks for meeting me," I said when I joined him, noticing he looked his usual devastatingly handsome self in a light charcoal grey suit and yellow silk tie.

His eyes regarded me with an indefinable emotion I could not understand but hoped wasn't pity. "Coffee?" he asked, and I nodded.

He ordered from the waitress, who of course made a beeline for him, and then he turned his attention back to me. "I'm glad you called," he remarked, and my heart skipped with joy. Perhaps, he had missed me.

Don't be ridiculous! Mike Connor loves Gina. But I love Mike, and he doesn't even know it. Dare I tell him? This is my one and only chance. If I leave this place without telling him how I truly feel, I will have lost him forever.

I couldn't meet his eyes for a few moments in case he saw the love reflected in my own. I desperately tried to find a way to tell him how much I loved him and took a few seconds to compose myself, being careful to focus my gaze on a point slightly above his eyebrow—but just as I was about to blurt out the whole truth, I chickened out and said instead, "I wanted to let you know that I'm going back to the UK in a couple of days' time." I hoped my voice sounded matter-of-fact. I thought I saw a fleeting look of disappointment in his eyes, though I couldn't be sure because I was too busy trying not to look directly into them.

"Then, you're not working at the bank anymore?" His voice

definitely held a tinge of disappointment in it, which gave me reason to hope.

Go on ... Tell him! Tell him before you change your mind. "It was a short-term assignment and it's finished now," I informed him, once again failing to say what I really wanted him to know.

"So what will you do back home?"

If only he didn't look at me with those beautiful eyes, full of green fire, and ask so many questions! I wanted to tell him I couldn't live without him, but fear of rejection kept rearing its ugly head. How could I face him if he said that while he was flattered I loved him, he couldn't return my feelings? Better to stay quiet then.

I shifted uncomfortably in my seat and was saved momentarily by the arrival of our coffees. I took my time stirring sugar into my cup and hoped the tears I felt at the back of my eyes would wait until I had a chance to say what I came to say, and then make a quick getaway.

"I'm going back to think about things," I finally spoke. Then, "The thing with Jeffrey's over and done with. Looking back now, I know it was just a bad infatuation on my side." There! If that wasn't a huge hint, what was? I dared to look into his eyes and was sure there was a brightness in them that could only mean one thing. My heart stopped.

"Sarah ..." He reached out with his hand and placed it on top of mine. I held my breath, waiting to hear what he would say next. This is it! This is the moment of truth. He will either tell me he loves me or he'll simply wish me luck with the rest of my life, I told myself, and felt my heart thumping crazily.

Mike's hand gave mine a gentle squeeze. "Sarah ..." He started again, but before he could continue, a female voice interrupted him.

"Mike, at last!" Gina remarked brightly and gave him a smile that I, in a shocked state, interpreted as sexy. "They told me you were in a meeting, but I urgently need to go over some figures with you."

She didn't even excuse herself for interrupting us nor did she acknowledge me. I was grateful for this, though, because I was too busy trying to compose myself and was therefore thankful she didn't look my way.

Mike sighed with exasperation, and I stole a quick look at his face in time to see annoyance written across it.

"Whatever it is, it can wait," he uttered in a low, but firm voice.

"I'll see you back at the office in half an hour."

By this time, I had recovered enough to feel the whole situation had been ruined by Gina's arrival. Not only this, but I was suddenly reminded she was the woman with whom Mike was going out. In fact, as far as I was concerned, he may have been getting ready to let me down gently when he was so rudely interrupted by her. In retrospect, Gina's arrival hadn't ruined anything at all. Perhaps, it was my salvation.

With this thought firmly implanted in my head, I grabbed the opportunity to make my escape. "It's okay, Mike," I interjected and stood up. "I think we're finished here." *In more ways than one.* "Besides, I need to go home and pack."

Now, I had Gina's full attention, but her smile was insincere. "Oh, forgive me, Sarah, for interrupting your meeting. I didn't know you were leaving so soon."

I managed to smile at the woman, who would one day bear Mike's children, and hoped to God that my eyes managed to hold back my tears. "Yes. I leave in a couple of days." Then, I turned to Mike. "Thank you for everything, Mike. I appreciate all the help you gave me. So … Well … Goodbye." My voice sounded croaky with emotion. "If you'll excuse me," I said to no one in particular; and I walked out of the café as if the hounds of hell were after me.

CHAPTER 21

I ate a sandwich for dinner that evening and decided to make a start on my packing. Monica had invited me to a fundraiser she was attending on behalf of her bank, but the chances of running into Mike were too high and I begged off. Besides, after the emotions of the afternoon, when I'd left him at the café, I was exhausted and wanted nothing but to sort through the things I would be taking back home.

"I'm leaving now," called Monica from the doorway. "Are you sure you won't change your mind?"

"Positive," I replied. "Have fun." When I saw the look in her eyes as she regarded me, I added, "Don't worry about me. I'll be fine." I forced a smile for her benefit.

"Okay. I may be back late, so don't wait up." She glanced at me one last time as if she wanted to say something else but seemed to change her mind, and she put on her coat instead.

I wished her a good evening and luxuriated in the feeling of having her lovely apartment to myself for a few hours. I took one look at the mound of clothes on my bed, waiting to be sorted through, and decided they could wait a little longer. What I needed right now was a nice long bath with some of Monica's imported bath oils.

I lay back in the bathtub enjoying the peace and quiet around me while I replayed in my mind the events of the afternoon. After I'd made my escape from the café, I had come straight home for a good cry in my room. Thankfully, Monica was at work, and the housekeeper on her day off. I tried to imagine my life without Mike, but all I saw was a big, black nothing, looming on the horizon. Mike had asked what I was going to do back home, and the answer was I had absolutely no idea. I planned to get a job as soon as possible, probably go back to teaching. Beyond this, I didn't know.

Now, as I started to relax in the bath, I asked myself what someone did when their whole life fell apart. They started all over again, I thought, feeling depressed. Despite my emotions, this was exactly what I intended to do. I would get a new job and a new flat— as soon as I could afford rent—and a new heart, although this last item would be very difficult to come by. They didn't exactly sell them on any street corner. I smiled sadly through the tears, which rose to my eyes, and I allowed them to fall unchecked into the bath water.

I wasn't sure how long I cried, nor did I care. I felt I deserved to wallow in self-pity for a little while, but my pity party didn't last very long for I suddenly became aware of a noise coming from the front door.

My head jerked up in attention. There was definitely someone out there. Perhaps, Monica had forgotten something and had come back for it. I quickly stepped out of the bath and threw on my bathrobe.

Slowly, I made my way to the front foyer and listened. Someone was fiddling with keys on the other side of the door, and it couldn't possibly be Monica because she knew exactly which key to use. Oh, God! Someone was trying to break in. I felt alarm as I bolted to my room, locked the door behind me, and rushed to the telephone. To my horror, I realised I couldn't remember the emergency number for the police in Hong Kong. In fact, I couldn't even think clearly through my fear; and before I could come up with a plan of action, I heard the front door open and someone walking in.

What now? I was twenty floors up from street level, so I couldn't very well jump off the balcony. In a moment of irony, I thought about Moira, always threatening to jump, and how she would have loved this particular scenario.

Before I could decide on what to do, my attention was diverted when the knob of my bedroom door began to turn. My throat went dry and I knew that even if I screamed, no one would hear me.

So this was the end, I thought glumly. Someone had broken in, and when they found me they would kill me, and I would never get to see Mike again. I would never be able to tell him I loved him. Why didn't I tell him when I had the chance? Now, it was too late. The thoughts rushed through my mind while I felt rising panic, watching the doorknob turn more insistently.

I was about to scream, even though I knew it would be futile, and nearly jumped out of my skin when there was a loud knock at the door.

"Sarah, if you're in there, open up!" It was Mike.

I sighed with relief while I wondered how he had gotten into the apartment, but this would have to wait. Instead, I tightened the belt around my bathrobe and went to unlock the door on unsteady legs. When I saw him standing there, so sexy in his tux, my legs almost buckled from under me—and they would have, except Mike reached out and pulled me to him.

"You little fool!" was all he said before his mouth came down on mine with such force I didn't know what hit me.

He kissed me with unleashed passion while his hands explored every inch of me, and the bathrobe fell to my feet. I felt I'd been transported to heaven and clung to him, no longer caring what he thought. Nothing seemed to matter through the onslaught of his mouth and hands on my body. All I could do was feel the wonderful sensations and press myself even closer to him.

Without breaking the kiss, he somehow maneuvered us toward the bed, and we fell on the pile of clothes I had been sorting through earlier. His kiss brought me to such a height of desire I moaned and felt my every limb melt. I couldn't get enough and knew I wanted him inside me. My hands made futile attempts to rip his clothes from him, but I was getting nowhere. I managed to slip a hand inside the waistband of his pants and when I made contact with his skin, he suddenly froze and slowly put me from him.

I wanted to scream for him not to reject me. Not again. Not this time. But Mike was already retrieving my robe from the floor and handing it to me. "Put this on. I can't talk to you when you look as you do now," he said roughly, his eyes full of passion when he looked at me.

I felt a rush of heat rise to my face and quickly scrambled into the robe while he straightened his clothes.

"Can we talk in the lounge?"

I nodded, dumbfounded, and felt the heat subside and the start of a chill take over my entire body. So much so, that I was shivering as I followed him out to the lounge room where we sat on the soft leather sofa facing each other.

"I'm sorry," Mike explained, now more in control of his emotions. "I came here with the intention of talking to you, but instead I find myself pawing you like a demented teenager." He threw me a smile of amusement.

I grinned at the picture this conjured up in my mind but could not control the shivering in my body. Here it comes, I thought. He's about to tell me he's going to marry Gina and wants me to be the first to know. But first, he's going to apologise for having lost control. I waited anxiously for the axe to fall.

"You're shivering," he stated, placing a warm hand on my shoulder. "Let me make you a hot drink."

"No!" I found my voice. "No. I'm okay. What … What … I mean, how did you get in here?" There were a million other questions I wanted to ask, but this was the most neutral one I could come up with.

"Monica gave me her keys at the function."

"You were at the fundraiser?" I asked stupidly, as if I didn't know.

"Yes. I was expecting you to be there. I wanted to talk to you about this afternoon," he answered. "I'm so sorry about Gina's interruption. She had no right to do that; and then you took off so quickly, I didn't get a chance to follow you."

"I said all I needed to say, so I just left," I remarked, but couldn't hide the pain in my voice at his mention of Gina.

I wondered why he was taking so long to tell me about his forthcoming marriage to her and didn't think I could stand the torture of hearing the words come out of his mouth. However, the fact that he had come here tonight, leaving the fundraiser where the undoubtedly lovely Gina waited alone, intrigued me.

I felt Mike's fingers under my chin as he lifted my face so he could look into my eyes. His own were a tempestuous green while he gazed into mine intently; and I gasped with fear when he took hold of my hands. This was the moment of truth.

"Sarah," he uttered gravely. "Stop playing games and be honest with me for once. Why did you want to see me today?"

I was momentarily surprised. He hadn't mentioned anything about Gina yet. "I …" I became lost in his gaze and couldn't focus on what I wanted to say. "I ..."

"You what?" he prompted gently, drawing a little closer to me.

I swayed toward him and shut my eyes quickly. Too late! A tear escaped from under one eyelid. Mike leaned closer and kissed it softly away. The shock at what he did made my eyelids fly open, and it must have been then that he saw the love reflected in my eye because he gasped—and he couldn't hide his expression quickly enough. Realising this, I tried to pull away so I could rearrange my thoughts at his discovery, but he would not release me. I felt miserable, and there was no doubt in my mind that he knew exactly how I felt about him.

"I'm still waiting for your answer," he reminded me as if the look in my eyes had not been enough.

I looked away from him and finally spoke in a soft voice. "I wanted to say goodbye because I was going back home."

He shook me gently, and I glanced back at him. The colour of his eyes was once again the sea green I so loved, and all of a sudden it didn't matter anymore that he might reject me. I felt like I was standing at the edge of a cliff about to fall over and spiral down to my death. Even if this were the case, I wanted him to know the truth about my feelings. At the risk of rejection and the pain it would bring, I still needed for him to know how I felt. True love was given unconditionally, without expectation; and this was my gift to the man I loved. I wanted to give of myself wholly without asking for anything in return.

I therefore gazed at him with loving eyes and declared in a firm and clear voice, "I wanted to see you to tell you I love you."

Through the fresh tears that gathered in my eyes, I finally saw what I had dreamed of a thousand times since I discovered my love for him—I saw a look of such love coming from his eyes, it took my breath away.

"Oh, my love," he murmured, close to my mouth. "How I hoped you'd say that." Then, he was kissing me, but this time it was a soft and slow kiss, a kiss that held the promise of a lifetime together with many wonderful things to come.

When he finally lifted his mouth from mine, I was beaming. "You love me? You don't think I'm on the rebound anymore? You're not with Gina?" I queried with incredulity.

He laughed and kissed me again, proving to me that yes, he loved me; no, he didn't think I was on the rebound; and no, he was definitely not with Gina.

"You don't know how crazy you made me," he confessed after kissing me once again thoroughly. "When we made love, I wanted so much to tell you how I felt; even back in London, when you thought I was rejecting you. I was so mad you were throwing yourself away on that good for nothing ..." He paused. I looked at him, puzzled; and he explained, "You wanted me to make love to you in London because you wanted to obliterate the memory of Jeffrey from your mind, but I couldn't do it under those circumstances. I wanted you to love me as much as I loved you. I didn't want you on the rebound."

"You loved me even then?" I gazed at him in wonder and my heart screamed with joy. Why hadn't I seen or felt this? *Because I'd been blind!* My infatuation with Jeffrey had blinded me for so long, I almost lost the true love of my life. The thought made me shiver.

Mike brought me closer to him. "I think I've loved you ever since I met you at Monica's Christmas party," he disclosed.

I was delighted. "What? But I ... But you ..."

"I know you don't remember much of what happened that night," he said with amusement. "You were under the weather. But when I saw you there, singing some silly song on karaoke, you were so adorable even when tipsy, that I lost my heart." He smiled lovingly. "I asked Monica who you were, and she told me you were in love with some guy called Jeffrey and that there were problems between you. She mentioned something about Moira and how all this time you'd been waiting for him to dump her."

I couldn't believe it. Mike had loved me from the very beginning, and all this time he'd been hiding his feelings so well. The rat! The charming, lovable, wonderful, sexy, devastatingly good looking, adorable rat. Now, my rat!

My heart sang with the knowledge he loved me, and I pressed even closer into his arms. "So this is why you agreed to help me," I accused him gently. "And I thought you were a smug womaniser who was in for the ride."

"You know I'd never do that, my love." He kissed my forehead. "I thought I could get to know you better if I agreed to help you, and I'd also get the chance to keep an eye on you. I guess I hoped in time you would develop feelings for me. I wanted you to realise you were going after the wrong boyfriend and wasting yourself on someone who didn't deserve you. But you were so determined to break up

Jeffrey and Moira that I felt I needed to pull away from you. Then, after we made love, I thought if I left you alone for a time, you might come to your senses and begin to see Jeffrey for what he really was."

"Well, I did come to my senses. I'm only sorry I took so long to do it," I replied with a contrite smile. "I was such a fool to think I could force someone to change, someone who didn't want to change. He was all wrong for me and yet I kept chasing him, and in the process I almost lost you."

"You thought you loved him, Sarah, and that he loved you, but I'm glad you didn't lose me."

I kissed him softly on the lips and confessed, "I didn't know what true love was until the day I told you about Jeffrey stealing my business—and you were so non-committal about things. You offered me help and showed concern, but you didn't say anything about your feelings. That's when I knew I loved you, but all you offered me was friendship and I was devastated."

"That's all I could offer you at the time," he replied. "I thought you were devastated because Jeffrey didn't return your love. So how could I come out and tell you I loved you?"

"I know," I agreed. "I know this now, but you didn't call me after that time, and I thought you didn't care at all. I thought the friendship you offered me was just you being nice to me. So I came back to Hong Kong and was miserable. Monica pretty much guessed straight away that I loved you. I ended up confessing everything to her and she tried to convince me to tell you about my feelings, before it was too late. But by this time, Gina was in the picture, and …well... you know."

Mike sat up straight, surprise in his eyes. "Gina again. When you mentioned her earlier, I thought you were asking if I was dating her casually, and the answer is I'm not, and never was."

"You mean you don't know about the gossip?" I regarded him with astonishment. "People said you relocated back to Hong Kong because of her. They said you two were an item." I relived the pain I felt when I had first heard this, and I gently placed my hand on Mike's chest to make sure I wasn't dreaming and that I was indeed sitting next to him with his arms around me. I had to know this whole thing wasn't just a fantasy inside my head.

Mike laughed, and I stared at him questioningly. "Don't look so confused, my love," he uttered. "It's just that it's so ironic. I came back to Hong Kong because this is where you are. Once you'd gone, I couldn't stay in Taipei a moment longer. All I wanted was to be close to you. So I decided to transfer Gina to Taipei and come back here. This is the only reason why I've been spending so much time with her lately. There was a lot we had to cover before she took over from me."

"But …" I was speechless.

Mike took the opportunity to kiss me once again, and we didn't talk for a long while. Much later, with our limbs interlocked, lying on the sofa, we continued talking. "It seemed everywhere I went, I ran into you and Gina," I recounted. "Plus people said she reminded you of Gloria, and that you were with her because you were thinking of marrying her and having a family—things you couldn't do with Gloria."

"You should know better than to listen to idle gossip," Mike rebuked me gently, "But they were right in one respect. I do want to marry one day, but Gina's not the girl I had in mind." The smile he gave me told me everything I needed to know.

"I love you so much, Mr Connor," I whispered, close to his mouth.

"And I love you, too, Ms Jamison, soon-to-change-your-last-name."

"Is that supposed to be a proposal?" I teased, but knew the answer even before he spoke.

"I know you're going to marry me," he asserted, kissing my lips gently.

I pulled back, pretending to be affronted. "You're overconfident, a charming rat, and very smug; you know that?"

"I know, but you love me all the same." He smiled and went to kiss me.

"Wait." I sat up suddenly and felt a little of my happiness ebb away.

Mike regarded me with curiosity. "What is it?"

"Mike, what if … I mean … well … the thing is …" I wasn't sure how to go on.

"You can tell me anything you like. You know I love you, and nothing else matters," he reassured me and pulled me back in his arms.

I rested my head on his chest. "It's about children. You know

157

I'm no longer that young … So what if …" I heard laughter and as I looked up at him, I saw the merriment in his eyes.

"Do you really think I won't marry you if you can't have children? What kind of a strange idea is that?" He seemed genuinely confused.

"But you said someday you wanted to live in the country and raise a family," I reminded him.

He caressed my face with his fingers and kissed the tip of my nose. "Sarah, while I would love to have children, not having any isn't going to stop me from loving you. You're my family now and wherever we go, we'll be together. And that's all I need."

Music to my ears! This was all I needed to know and before I could say anything else, his mouth covered mine—and there was no more to be said.

The End

About The Author

Sylvia Massara is a multi-genre author based in Sydney, Australia. She loves to dabble in wacky love affairs, drama, murder, sci-fi (or anything else that takes her fancy) over good coffee.

Born in Argentina from Italian and Spanish descent (with a bit of Swiss thrown in) and transplanted to Australia at age 10, Sylvia describes herself as a bit of a "moggie" cat by way of mixed pedigree. She is also a citizen of the world as she has travelled widely throughout most of her life and she's the proud owner of three passports.

From a creative perspective, Sylvia has been writing since her early teens and her work consists of novels, screenplays and freelance writing. She has also dabbled in acting on and off, songwriting and even had her own band during her teens/early 20s where she performed at various venues.

As with most authors, Sylvia draws on her varied experience from the often puzzling tapestry of life. A few years ago Sylvia resigned from the human race because she discovered the animal kingdom was a much nicer place to be.

Currently, Sylvia lives with her cat, Mia; and always vicariously through the many characters in her head. Occasionally, Sylvia ventures into the world of humans, and she cherishes genuine friendships as they are a rare find.

Sylvia has recently released her 7th novel, The Stranger, a sci-fi apocalyptic romance with moralistic issues that involve the fight of love vs evil in the cosmos.

Please visit the author's website to keep up with her latest novels or to contact her at: www.sylviamassara.com

About Massara's Novels

The Mia Ferrari Mystery Series

<u>Playing With The Bad Boys</u>

A woman plunges ten floors down an atrium and lands on a baby grand piano in the luxurious Rourke Hotel Sydney. The police rule this as a straight case of suicide; but 48-year-old hotel duty manager and wannabe investigator, Mia Ferrari, thinks otherwise.

As Mia sets out to unravel the mysterious death and prove the cops wrong, especially her archenemy, Detective Sergeant Phil Smythe; she comes up against an unsavoury cast of characters who will do anything to shut her up. But with a little help from her friends, Mia will not stop until she unearths the truth.

Mia Ferrari is a "wiseass", older chick with determination and an attitude, and she never takes "no" for an answer.

<u>The Gay Mardi Gras Murders</u>

Mia Ferrari, smartarse, older chick, super sleuth, is back in her 2nd murder mystery, and this time, she is up to her neck in drag queens, a rare diamond with a curse and murder most foul against the backdrop of Sydney's world famous Gay Mardi Gras.

A female impersonator is found dismembered in her hotel suite bathtub, and a rare diamond worth twenty million dollars is gone. The Gay Mardi Gras is fast approaching and Mia Ferrari, senior duty manager of the exclusive Rourke International Hotel Sydney, has to juggle a bunch of drag queens, a number of fabulously handsome gay men, a transsexual with a dark mystery, a young cop with sex on his mind, a close friend from the UK who is having marital problems and a mounting body count.

As Mia pits her investigative skills against her archenemy, Detective Sergeant Phil Smythe, to solve the case, she not only becomes embroiled in the life of the people around her, but it looks like she is the next target for a serial killer with a grudge against gay men.

The South Pacific Murders

It's a well-known fact that wherever Mia Ferrari goes trouble always follows, and going on a holiday cruise to Hawaii is no different.

A killer is on the loose onboard ship. A number of doctors from a medical convention are being murdered one by one. The captain of the cruise liner asks Mia and her travelling companions to take over the investigation while the ship is in the middle of the Pacific Ocean toward its final destination. A secret sex club and horse racing bets are the only clues that can uncover the identity of the killer, but will Mia be able to solve the mystery before the killer strikes again?

Join Mia and her friends, plus her sexy detective archenemy, on a cruise to murder, mayhem, and sizzling hot sex.

Sci-fiction romance

The Stranger

The Stranger is a sci-fi apocalyptic romance with moralistic issues involving the fight between love and evil and its repercussions.

Rhys is on a mission on Earth in order to determine Earth's destiny, but his judgement is in danger of becoming clouded when he meets and falls in love with Carla, a human. The balance of life on Earth depends upon Rhys's recommendation to the League of Galaxies. But how will Rhys choose between his mission and his love for an Earthling? Rhys is forced to weigh up the collective evil on Earth and its causal effect on the greater good of other life in the universe against the love he has for one woman.

This is not simply a tale of love between two beings but a story of the unconditional and sublime love, which is the force that drives the cosmos.

The Stranger was dedicated to the Loving Memory of David Bowie.

Romantic Comedy

Like Casablanca

What does internet dating and Casablanca have in common? Nothing, unless you go to Rick's Cafe and find out what antiques dealer and dating blogger, Cat Ryan, is up to.

Cat's doing research for her internet dating blog gig, and the place she chooses to meet her many dates is at Rick's Cafe in Sydney. But what of its disturbingly handsome owner, Rick Blake?

Cat wonders what he thinks, seeing her with a different male all the time. What's more, why does this bother Cat so much? It's not like she wants any involvement after her recent break up with Josh, her cheating ex. Besides, it looks like Rick is trying to get back together with his ex-wife, Denise. So Cat decides to play it safe, but her heart has different ideas.

The Other Boyfriend

Sarah Jamison is on a mission to find a boyfriend for Moira, who is her lover's partner. And Sarah's best friend, Monica, comes to the rescue with the perfect solution. Enter the enigmatic Mike Connor.

Monica is sure that Mike will sweep Moira off her feet, leaving the way open for Sarah to be with her true love, Jeffrey.

Sarah hates Mike on sight despite the fact that her body tells her otherwise. He is a romance novel "hero-type" who is smug and full of himself. But the only way to accomplish her mission is for her to work with Mike so she can be together with the man she loves.

Jeffrey has promised her that the minute he can end his platonic relationship with Moira, he will be with Sarah for good; but he is having trouble letting go of the wretched woman, and Sarah feels her time is running out. She is terrified of the pending big "M" (menopause), and seeing as she's just turned forty, and her hormones are driving her to do insane and desperate things, she is sure that it is not too far off into the future!

So here she is, building a multi-level marketing business in Taiwan, and struggling with it all: a stranger in a foreign country, away from her mother and friends back in London; a reluctant lover; a drop-dead gorgeous man who might have ulterior motives for helping her, and finally, a business that seems to be dwindling.

Sarah is doing it all in the name of love and the last chance to have a family, and if this means scheming and working with the devil himself, then she will do it! What she doesn't take into account is the fact that instead of getting closer to her goal, Sarah's feelings take a turn, and she finds herself increasingly thinking about the very man she despises the most – "the other boyfriend".

Contemporary fiction - drama

The Soul Bearers

Partly inspired by true life events, this is a story of courage, the gift of friendship, and unconditional love. The story involves three people whose lives cross for a short period of time and the profound effect that results from their interaction.

Alex, a freelance travel writer and victim of child abuse, arrives in Sydney in an attempt to exorcise the ghosts of her past. She shares a house with Steve and the disturbing Matthew, a homosexual couple. Alex finds herself inexplicably attracted to Matthew and she must battle with her repressed sexuality and fear of intimacy. Matthew, an aspiring actor, must face the prospect of a potential future without his partner, who has AIDS, and he must deal with the rejection of his socialite parents.

Steve is the rock to which the troubled Matthew and Alex cling while they examine their lives and beliefs in the hope that they will find the strength to face their pain and release the past.

This powerful story explores the true meaning of unconditional love and friendship.